Age-old Enemies

Danielle Paquette-Harvey

1984 –

Cover by Jennifer Givner

ISBN 978-1-7775721-3-6 (paperback)

First Edition: September 2021

Published by: Danielle Paquette-Harvey

http://daniellephauthor.com

https://www.instagram.com/daniellephauthor

Subscribe to my mailing list so you don't miss anything!

daniellephauthor.com

Follow me
- Facebook: Danielle Paquette-Harvey author
- Instagram: daniellephauthor

Other books by the author
Prequel to this series
- The prophecy (*available on amazon*)
  ISBN 978-1777572105

Longing mates Series

1. Age-Old Enemies (*available on amazon*)
   ISBN 978-1777572136

2. A Beloved Sin (*available on amazon*)

ISBN 978-1777572150

Danielle Paquette-Harvey

Age-old Enemies

Prologue

Fog was settling at ground level. I felt the freshness of the dew on my feet, walking in the balmy summer night. In the sky, the moon was full, bathing nature in its soft light. In the air lingered the earthy smell of rain on grass from the light showers that fell earlier. I made my way silently towards the shapes in the mist, hiding myself in a nearby bush. Behind the shadows slept the peaceful water of a lake. I was scared but too curious to go away.

"Did someone see you?" asked the man.

"No, don't worry, nobody saw me," answered the woman.

"Good, do you have it?" Without answering, the woman took something from her bag.

"Here it is … are you sure about this?"

The man seemed to ponder for a moment. "It's the only way."

The woman nodded before hugging the man.

"I will be back here in a week of time from now, you have my promise." He kissed her tenderly.

"You'd better be, you know what would happen if anyone would find out it was missing."

The man had a serious face. He only answered, "I know."

I didn't really understand what was going on, but I knew there wasn't supposed to be any witnesses of this encounter. I had the feeling I knew this man, but I couldn't see him clearly with all the fog, despite having an advanced sense of vision at night. His scent was familiar too. I also had an advanced sense of smell, but it was not fully developed, since I was so young.

As I tried to get closer to them, a firefly came on the tip of my nose, making it itch, making me sneeze.

"Achoo!"

At the noise of my sneezing, the woman took a step back, gasping. The man took a step in my direction asking in a threatening tone, a growl escaping his chest.

"Who's there?"

I was scared but I knew it was too late to try to hide. I couldn't run away; I was not fast enough. They would catch me for sure. I took a few steps in their direction, my heart racing, and showed myself to them.

Coming into the moonlight, I said shyly, "It's only me."

Now that I was closer to them, I could see them both clearly. I recognized the man to be Uncle Zach. I felt relieved.

"Hi Uncle Zach."

I looked at him, smiling. His face softened as he looked down at me and the woman eased herself.

"Hey Kate, you are up late today little lady," he said to me in a teasing voice. "Do your parents know you are out here?"

I think he was worried more people would come by and find about his meeting with the mysterious woman. I shook my head.

"I'm a big girl now you know... But... You won't tell them I sneaked out, right?"

Zach laughed at my question.

"Hum … let's see… You're right, you are a big girl now. Five years old is really big so… What do you say we make this our little secret?"

Zach winked. I've always loved Uncle Zach; he was the best.

I felt relieved by his proposition. I didn't want to get in trouble for sneaking out again. Happy, I nodded and gave him a big hug.

Then I turned my head to look at the woman standing beside him.

"Is this your friend?" They both smiled at my question.

Zach answered, "you could say that."

I looked at her, she was very beautiful. She had straight long black as ebony hair and her skin was white as snow. Her lips were red as blood and her eyes had a golden glow to them.

I didn't recall ever seeing her before. Her scent had something special in it, but I didn't know what it was. I've never smelled someone like her.

I mean I've smelled both werewolves and humans in the past, but she wasn't either, so I wasn't sure exactly what she was.

"Will she come and play at our house tomorrow? She looks nice."

She kneeled to my level. "I'm afraid that's not possible right now my dear…"

I felt disappointed by her answer. I guess it showed on my face since she added quickly, "But maybe soon it will be."

Hearing her say that made my smile reappear. She truly looked nice, and I hoped we could be friends. I gave her a big hug, which seemed to take her by surprise at first, but then she returned my hug. Her skin felt cool to the touch, I liked her. I hoped she'd come and visit us sometimes.

Zach looked at me. "Well, it's time you get to bed, little lady."

"Aww… But I don't want to." I protested pouting my lips.

I didn't want to admit it, but I was becoming tired. Even if I wanted to stay awake, staying up was getting harder and harder. My eyelids seemed to get heavier, and I still had to walk all the way to my house.

Reluctantly I told him, "Okay … you're right."

"You'd better get home before your parents realize you are gone," the woman added with a wink. I nodded to them.

Zach cupped the woman's face in his hand and kissed her lovingly. The way he looked at her would make the moon jealous. It was like she was the most precious treasure in the world.

"I will see you soon my love," he told her.

"I will be waiting."

Zach took my hand. "Shall we get going?"

I yawned and nodded while rubbing my sleepy eyes. We walked back to the house; Zach carrying me the last few steps as I was too tired to walk.

Everything was silent, the lights were closed. Zach tucked me into my bed before going to his room. My thoughts wandered to the woman I saw tonight as I let myself drift to sleep. Who was she? I didn't even think about asking for her name. What was it that she gave to Uncle Zach? I guess I could ask him tomorrow but for now, I was just too tired and couldn't resist slumber.

Chapter 1 (Kate)

A Summer's vacation

Eighteen years later

I opened my eyes. The rays of the sun seeped through the blinds of the windows. I could already smell the scent of fresh coffee coming from downstairs.

I got up and dressed myself. This was the first day of my vacation. I worked as an accountant in downtown Montréal. I loved my job, but I was overdue for vacation! This was going to be a great day!

I couldn't wait to go into the woods. As I exited my room, I saw Bianca also getting out of her room. She looked as excited as I was.

"Hey Sis," she said smiling at me. "He's sleeping late again."

She was pointing to our brother's room.

I laughed. Will was always sleeping late. He had to take classes at night to become leader of the pack's elite protectors one day. He was already one of the strongest wolves of the pack. And the fact that our father was the Alpha meant Will was even stronger and bigger than most of the other wolves.

Our parents had high hopes for him. But because of that, he was always staying up really late at night. So of course, when morning came, he had a hard time getting up.

I thought he trained too much but he always said that you have to be prepared for anything, you never know what might happen. I know he gives it all he has, taking his protector role seriously.

Even though, I knew he wouldn't be happy if we went without him. I told my sister, "I'll get him up, you go and get breakfast ready, okay?"

Bianca nodded before heading to the kitchen.

I entered my brother's room and tried to wake him up gently.

"Hey sleepyhead. It's time to wake up."

He turned to his side and growled, " ... let me sleep."

I shrugged my shoulders. "Suit yourself. We'll be going to the forest soon to see Steven anyways."

At those words I heard him sigh. Will opened his eyes. "Right, I forgot about that."

Steven was our cousin. It was his birthday; he was turning eighteen today and we all agreed to go hangout together in the forest like when we were kids. Eighteen was an important age for wolves as we officially became of age and could therefore find our mates. Although most of us didn't find their mates until later in life.

Will especially loved to fight with Steven, as he was also one of the strongest wolves of the pack. He was a great training opponent. After all, his mother, our aunt Suzan, also had Alpha blood in her veins. Even if she wasn't the leader of the pack, she was still stronger than most of the pack's members.

I looked at my little brother, who was not so little anymore, now being twenty-one years old and almost six feet tall. With all his training, he was becoming quite handsome. He would make a she-wolf happy one day. But to me, he was my little brother that I loved.

"Right, then I'll see you downstairs for breakfast."

He smiled at me. "Okay sis, I'm coming. Wait for me before you go out."

I went down to the kitchen. My mother and father were talking with Bianca. My mother Sarah still looked young and beautiful, not yet in her fifties. My dad, Sam, was still a strong Alpha. I loved my parents. Even though I had my apartment in Montréal, I always spent all my vacations at my parent's domain, with the rest of the pack. As werewolves, it was important to stick together and protect one another.

My brother was an exact copy of my father; tall, broad muscled chest, dark brown hair, but he got blue eyes instead of the green of our father's eyes. And I was an exact copy of my mother; short, brown hair and hazel eyes.

Nobody really knew who my sister Bianca took after. She had long blond almost white hair and deep piercing ice blue eyes. As far as anyone could tell, she was human, like my mom. She was now twenty years old. She didn't change into a wolf even once.

Usually, lycanthrope like us turn for the first time when they get to twelve or fourteen years old max. But Bianca never turned, and she didn't have any sign she would be changing into a wolf anytime soon. It was believed she didn't get the lycanthrope genes. Unlike my brother and me. We got it from our father. We didn't speak too much about that since we knew she still hoped she would turn to a wolf one day.

Breakfast was already on the table and a cup of hot dark roasted coffee awaited me. The scent of coffee mixed with the scent of eggs seemed irresistible. I hugged my parents before digging into my plate. Soon after, my brother came down as well and devoured his breakfast. As soon as we were all done, we excused ourselves and set to the forest.

Normally, when Will and I go to the forest together, we would change into our wolf's form, since it goes way faster to run into the forest this way rather than on two legs. Plus, when in your wolf's form, you get that freedom feeling and the wind blowing through your fur.

Since Bianca was there with us today, we'd stay into our human form. We wouldn't want her to feel left out.

We ran together, knowing very well the path to our favorite hangout place, near the river. The sun was shining bright and warm, birds were singing in the trees.

Getting close to the river, I could see in the distance a big white wolf with blue eyes. It was Steven, he got there before us. There was not a lot of white wolves around here, but Steven's father was one, and he inherited it from him.

Bianca's cheeks turned red. I knew she loved to see Steven's wolf and he was well aware of it too. He was doing it on purpose as often as he could, making her blush every time. He liked to show off.

Even if he was our cousin, I knew Bianca had a crush on him. I didn't worry about it too much as none of us had found our mates yet. The day it would happen she would lose all interest in Steven as he would lose all interest in her too.

As we approached, Steven got behind a bush and changed back to his human form. He took a bag next to him and dressed himself.

When we changed from our wolf form to our human form, we would be completely naked, so we always kept a change of clothes hidden in the woods nearby. He was completely dressed when we arrived by his side.

"Hey Steven! Happy birthday!" I told him, giving him a hug.

"Yo, happy birthday bro," Will told him giving him a pat on the shoulder. They did this kind of weird man's secret handshake finishing with a fist bump. I had seen them do it numerous times but failed to remember the movements every time.

Steven looked at Bianca. She was standing timidly in front of him. "Happy birthday, Steven."

He passed his fingers through his hair. "Thanks guys! I'm so glad to see you."

We all sat facing the river, at our usual spot. Bianca next to Steven, then Will and then me. All the four of us were enjoying the sun, talking and joking, just enjoying life. When we got together like that, I felt like I was back in my childhood; no worries, just enjoying life to its fullest.

The day was passing by fast; the guys went to hunt some prey for us to eat. Bianca and I picked up wood and started a fire while waiting for them to come back. I just loved the smell of fire and the crackle the wood makes while burning. When the guys came back, we roasted the meat on the fire and ate.

We didn't even notice the sun coming down. It got dark, but our night vision was good, thanks to our lycanthrope's genes. The moon was out in the sky and the stars were shining. We were laughing and talking, life was good.

"Hey Steven," Bianca said, "I have a little gift for you."

We all looked at her. She took out of her pocket a small charm.

"It's a good luck charm." It was shaped like the moon and hung from a string. "I made it myself," she added with a big smile.

Steven smiled back at her. "Then I'm sure it will bring me luck. Would you mind tying it around my neck please?"

I knew without looking that Bianca was probably blushing right now. She got up on her knees and proceeded to tie the charm around Steven's neck. As she did, she lost her balance. Steven put his arms around her waist, so she didn't fall.

I looked at my brother and said with a wink, "Hey Will, why don't you come with me, we'll go back to the house."

He looked at Bianca and Steven and smiled. "Yeah okay, you guys catch up with us later."
We didn't wait for a reply. I got up with my brother and we started walking back to the house.

As we walked, I started to wonder how it would be when I would finally find my mate. Will and I promised each other a long time ago we would tell each other when we found our mates, our perfect half, the one chosen by the moon goddess for us. So far, neither of us seemed to have found our mate.

"So Will, any sign of your mate yet?"

My brother looked at me. "No. You know I would have told you if it had been the case... But, in the meantime, I did get a date with that cute blondie wolf."

I sighed. "Not Marie?"

Will laughed. "What? What's wrong with her?"

I growled; I couldn't stand Marie. "You know I don't like her. Besides about half of the pack has seen her ass."

Will chuckled. "Well, I don't see any harm in having a little fun while I still haven't found my mate."

I laughed at his comment. "Yeah, I guess you're right," I admitted.

Even if I didn't like her, at least she wasn't his mate, which was a relief. Just imagine if I had to endure her forever.

Besides, it's not like I haven't dated anyone either. Some werewolves never find their mates. You never know when and if you are going to find it, so it's okay to enjoy yourself in the meantime.

I was thinking about all of that when a strange scent hit me. I stopped walking. I looked at Will and from the look he was giving, he smelled it too. It wasn't the scent of a wolf, neither a human. I wasn't quite sure what that scent was. Strangely, I felt like it wasn't the first time that I smelled it.

We looked around in silence, searching for where it was coming from. A shiver ran through my body, making the hair stand up on the back of my neck.

Suddenly, a man came out of the bush. He matched my brother in height and size. He had long brown hair with highlights going down the middle of his back, a trimmed beard and a small mustache.

The way he was looking at us, I knew he wasn't friendly. His eyes were red, and his skin was pale. Surely it was a vampire. But what was a vampire doing into our territory? This was a violation of the treaty.

"Run!" My brother shouted to me before changing into his wolf form.

Strangely, the man's gaze seemed to hypnotize me. As he looked at me, I could feel him staring at my soul. I knew I should get away or attack, but I could not move. For some reason, my wolf wanted to see him more, I felt drawn to him.

Will jumped on him, causing the man to break our eye contact that was mesmerizing me. As soon as I snapped out of it, I ran as fast as I could towards our home.

I was scared as hell and my heart was beating fast. I couldn't stop from asking myself if there were other vampires around. Would I be attacked while running? I tried to push away those thoughts and continued running as fast as I could, until my lungs hurt. Luckily for me, I arrived at our house a few minutes later.

When I entered the kitchen, my parents were both sitting on the couch. My father was reading a book. As soon as I entered the room, he lifted his eyes from it and looked at me. He could hear my panting and sense the panicked state I was in. I was shaking.

"What happened?" he asked anxiously.

"We were attacked!"

My mother stood up and ran to me. "Are you okay? Are you hurt sweetie?" she asked me.

"I'm fine." I told them, still catching my breath.

"What attacked you?" my father asked.

The question brought back everything that had happened and the image of the man vividly in my mind.

"It was a vampire. I saw his red eyes and pale skin."

My father growled. "Vampires! How dare they break the treaty! Where are the others?"

"Will was fighting him when I ran home. Bianca was with Steven at the river."

It hit me! We left Bianca and Steven behind! I hoped they were fine. Bianca couldn't change into a wolf, so she was vulnerable. Luckily, Steven was a strong fighter, he would protect her I was sure of it, or at least that's what I was trying to convince myself of.

With all the commotion, my uncle Zach came downstairs. He lived with us. Some of the important wolves of the pack also lived with us in the house. The rest of the pack was living in houses nearby. We stayed close one to another as we protected each other.

"What's going on?" he asked.

Without answering, my father changed into his wolf form.

My mother walked to open the door to let him out, but before she could, the door slammed open. Bianca and Steven came into the house.

Steven was holding an injured wolf. I could recognize this black wolf anywhere; it was my brother.

"Will!" I screamed as I went to see him.

He was injured but it didn't seem to be lethal.

If only I had stayed and fought with him, I told myself. I shouldn't have run home. I'm the worst big sister. Tears began coming down my cheeks.

Behind them, my mother closed and locked the door. I could hear my father changing back to his human form and Zach coming to see if Steven and Bianca were fine.

"Hey, hey what's the big drama?" a teasing voice asked.

I looked at Will. He was on the floor, in his human form.

I shouted at him, "hey you! Don't joke about stuff like that! You made me worry!"

I pouted my lips and threw a blanket to cover him up. Will laughed, still lying on the floor.

"I wasn't joking. I think my ankle is twisted or something. Steven carried me so we would escape the guy who attacked us."

"Did he hurt you?" my father asked him anxiously.

"He tried to bite me and scratch me with his nails."

My dad's face darkened as my brother continued, "but he disappeared before I could really hurt him."

"What the hell are they doing here?" asked my father with hatred, "Zach, we need to do an emergency council meeting right now!"

"Yes Sam, right away," Zach answered.

Zach went upstairs to gather some things. My father kneeled close to my brother.

"You are certain he didn't bite you?"

"Yes, I'm positive about that."

"Good, see you in my study then," replied my father before he went up.

I didn't know what to think. I had never seen a vampire before. Why was I so hypnotized by him? I couldn't attack him. I just kept staring. Even now, I remember his gaze so clearly. I could see my reflection in it. He seemed as mesmerized about my eyes as I was about his... But now was not the time to think about this, I reminded myself. We had urgent matters to deal with.

My brother was still lying on the floor with his sprained ankle. I hugged him tight.

"I'm so sorry I left you all alone."

I felt really bad, we should've stuck together. I should have been there for him.

"Don't worry about it, Sis. I wouldn't be a good brother if I let anything happen to my sister." He winked.

"Still, I should have stayed with you to fight." I threw him some clothes.

My brother looked at me and said teasingly after getting dressed, "Well, you didn't look like you were going to fight anytime soon anyway."

I didn't really know what to answer to that. It was as if I was hypnotized by the vampire. I felt even worse because of that. Not only did I run away, but I was frozen in place instead of attacking him.

"... Yeah, I know... I don't know what happened to me."

My brother shrugged his shoulders.

"No worries. We should get to the meeting."

He was right. As the Alpha's first child, I was the current Beta, the future Luna of the pack. The mate I would choose would become the future Alpha. It was an important role. I felt pressured to find a strong mate. I didn't really want the title, but I was the oldest. I would gladly give the title to my brother instead. So many responsibilities came with it. Still, I had to attend the meeting, and so did my brother and sister.

I helped my brother up. He passed his strong arm around my shoulder and limped a little. Even if his ankle hurt him, he stood fairly straight on his leg. As werewolves, we had healing powers. Being the Alpha's children, ours were more advanced than the other werewolves. I knew that in a matter of minutes his ankle would probably be fine. For the moment, I was happy to be there for him, letting him lean on me.

We went to my father's study. The lights gave a yellowish look to the room but at the same time it felt warm. A few of the pack's members were already there.

Steven was there, as one of the pack's lead fighters. Bianca was at his side. They stared at each other while waiting for everyone to arrive. Zach, one of the most trusted advisors of the pack, was there as well.

My father stood tall behind his sturdy wooden desk. He was studying everyone, mentally counting who was there and who was still missing from the meeting. My mother stood by his side, a hand on his shoulder. You could read tenderness in her eyes. My father would always get a little nervous when he needed to hold these kinds of meetings. She always managed to calm him; she was his rock in stressful moments.

I could hear murmurs all around us. People speculating as to why my father would call a meeting on such short notice at night.

When everyone got there, my father motioned for Zach to close the door. Everybody got silent, waiting for him to start talking. He didn't beat around the bush and got straight to the point. "We are gathered here because a vampire was seen in our territory."

A few people gasped and murmurs started to spread across the room. My father cleared his throat, waiting for silence to return. "As if breaking into our territory wasn't enough, he attacked my son."

A woman asked in fear, "what are we going to do? Do you have a plan?"

A few other questions started to rise here and there, mostly people inquiring as to what our riposte would be.

A young man raised his hand and asked, "Why would vampires attack us in the first place?"

My father looked at him with a stern face. "Did you sleep through your history classes?"

All eyes fell on the young man who suddenly turned as red as a beet.

My father sighed loudly. "For those of you who don't know, I think it's about time we remind you about our history."

Then he looked at Zach. "Would you care to?"

Zach gave a small bow at my father and took the lead.

"A few thousand years ago, vampires attacked us, trying to eliminate us. They considered werewolves were a threat, a competitor for their prey, the humans. They think lowly of us, thinking we are just beasts, animals. They loathe us. It was a ferocious war, and we were not strong enough. One by one, we were going down. We lost many packs of wolves to that war. At last, all the remaining packs united and fought back, everyone together, against the vampires. We were able to eliminate a lot of them. Finally, with both sides weakened and injured, a peace treaty was signed. It was agreed that we were to leave each other alone and not trespass on each other's territories."

"But tonight," continued my father with a strong voice, "this treaty has been broken by the vampires! Which means that war has been declared by our enemy! We must prepare ourselves and fight back!"

People started cheering all around us. I was shocked. I couldn't believe what I was hearing! A war with the vampires? This seemed all surreal to me. I didn't really listen to the rest of the rambling between the other pack members.

Suddenly, one of the lookouts barged into the room. "They are at the front door! We are being attacked!"

My father took a commanding voice. "We need you guys downstairs to defend ourselves. Bianca, Kate, Sarah, you girls go back to your rooms and lock your doors."

"What? I want to fight too!" I protested.

Nobody in their right mind would question the Alpha's authority. That is, unless you had a death wish. I really wanted to help defend my pack, as the alpha's daughter. As soon as I said the words, from the looks everyone gave me, I immediately regretted going against my dad's will. My father looked at me with a harsh look of alpha's authority. No one can resist the alpha's authority. I looked to the floor, bending myself a little.

"You will do as I say," my father growled at me.

I shyly replied without looking at him, "Yes Father." and started to get out of the room.

"Don't worry, Sis," my brother said to me in a low voice as I left with my mother, "I'll keep you safe."

The men started to get downstairs to fight off the vampires.

Bianca went directly to her room without question. I was walking slowly. I was pissed at my father. I walked back to my room with my mother. "Why can't I fight too? I have alpha blood, I can fight, it's not like I'm useless."

My mother sighed. "You know how your father wants to protect us. His wolf gets a little crazy when he's scared of losing the ones he loves. He used to do this when we dated, back then. He only does that because he loves you, my dear."

I knew she was right. Werewolves, especially the males, get very protective of their mate and families. You only have one mate for your whole life, chosen by the moon goddess. If they happen to die, you stay alone for the rest of your life, longing for your fallen mate. I've heard my father was quite protective of my mother before I was born. I didn't know all the details, but I've heard my mother was abducted and he came to rescue her.

"Yeah, I guess you're right. But still, I would like him to allow me to fight for the pack. I am the Beta. I want to be part of it and protect our people with my life."

My mother hugged me. "Don't worry my dear, you'll have your chance. Let your father protect you while he still can. One day he's going to get old and it's going to be your turn."

I smiled at her. She always knew how to comfort me. Mothers know best. I hugged her and entered my room. My mother continued to her own room, a little farther.

I entered my room. Sincerely I was a little exhausted from everything that had happened today. It was dark and I didn't bother to turn on the lights. The moon lit the room enough for me to see. As I walked to my bed, I could hear the commotion going on outside the house. I didn't really know if I would be able to sleep with the battle going on, but I guess I should at least try.

As I got close to my bed, something felt off. I felt the hair at the back of my neck rising. Then the smell hit me. It was the same smell as in the forest. He was close I was sure of it. But why did it smell so good? I spotted his red eyes in the corner of my room. He was mostly hiding in the shadow.

"I know you are here. Show yourself!" I said with as much authority I could, trying to hide my fear.

The vampire took a step into the moonlight. He looked to be about thirty years old, a few years older than me. He had a broad chest with muscles, dressed elegantly. He would be very handsome, if you passed over the fact that he was a bloodsucking parasite that could kill you. The moment I saw him, my heart started to beat faster, and my wolf wanted to come out. I guess the fear was taking a hold of me and I fought hard to try to calm myself down. He stared at me without moving, like in the forest earlier.

"What do you want from me?" I found myself hypnotized by his eyes again.

He answered with a low voice, "Please, I do not wish to harm you."

Strangely, I felt that he was telling the truth. I didn't really know how or why, but I felt drawn to him. Like I've never felt before. I've heard vampires could seduce their prey before sucking their blood. Was it his doing? I was fighting my whole body, reminding myself that he was the enemy. He was studying me, I felt like he was trying to look at my soul. None of us moved. My wolf wanted me to go to him. I was fighting myself not to listen to her.

Suddenly, a shadow moved in the other corner of my room. I startled and turned back to see another vampire coming my way.

"Now, now, now. When will you learn to stop playing with your prey?" he asked the first vampire.

Coming into the moonlight, this one had white short hair, he was taller and looked younger than the first vampire. But he looked meaner, I didn't trust him at all. My wolf growled threateningly.

The first vampire replied, "Careful, we're only here for the relic, do not harm her."

The second vampire laughed at his comment.

"While we're here, we might as well have a little fun," he said to the first vampire with a fake smile, before lunging an attack at me. I dodged his attack and pushed him back, but he threw me on the floor, keeping me down with the weight of his body.

I saw his nails start to grow and his fangs come out. He was going to attack me and drink my blood! Fear started creeping inside me. I couldn't let him kill me like that. My wolf snarled so hard it startled him. I let myself change into my wolf, my clothes ripping apart, despite having a vampire on top of me. I bit him hard on the arm and was able to get up to my feet. The vampire cursed and tried to scratch me with his nails, but I dodged his attacks.

Just as I thought I was getting the upper hand, the vampire cornered me. There was nowhere for me to go. He was definitely stronger than me. I growled violently at him, trying to hold my position.

Just when he was about to attack me, the first vampire stopped him.

"That is enough Arius!"

He pushed him out of the way and came in front of me.

The first vampire looked me in the eyes and said with a low voice, "forgive me."

Before I even had time to wonder what he meant by that, or why I didn't seem to be able to attack him, I blacked out.

Chapter 2 (Damien)

The prisoner

He wanted to kill her. I couldn't let him do this, so I set her unconscious. Why the hell did I do that? I have no idea. I was so angry at my stupid brother. Our goal was only to steal the werewolf's family heirloom, not to kill anyone. I guess that's why. When I saw my brother, ready to suck the life out of her, I just couldn't let him do it.

When I set her unconscious, she changed back to her human form. There she was, lying on the floor, naked. I couldn't help myself but to stare at her beauty for a moment. But then, as my brother got pissed at me for stopping him, I threw a blanket over her to hide her body. I grabbed her in my arms and flew away, before anyone else would enter her room.

There I was, flying back home, holding a naked she-wolf wrapped in a blanket in my arms. I knew I would have some questions to answer when we get back. I could sense very well the anger coming from my brother, flying a little further away from me. I had until I got home to come up with a damn good reason for not killing this girl and bringing her back with me. Father would kill me if I didn't.

I was lost in my thoughts as I flew. I was trying to find an excuse to tell everyone as we'd be back at the castle. Yet, all I could think about was her. I loved that fire in her eyes when she fought my brother. I kept thinking back at the way she looked at me when I saw her. I didn't use any kind of powers on her, so why is it she was staring at me like that? Still now, in my arms, unconscious, she looked like an angel. I could hear her breathing, even hear the blood pumping in her body.

As predators, our brains were wired to hear all that's related to blood and breathing of potential prey. But right now, it was a reassuring sound, knowing that she was alive, asleep in my arms… What was I thinking? She's our enemy, a beast, nothing more. I need to stay focused on my task, I reminded myself.

Shortly after, we arrived at the castle. The castle walls stood on top of a mountain. The walls were partly in white stucco and black bricks. The contrast gave a nice accent to the walls. It gave a Spanish look to the castle. The walls were quite high, and you could count up to six floors with the windows. On some floors were balconies. The vines growing from the ground would climb and reach to the balconies on the lower floors. It was a beautiful sight.

The base of the castle was built into the rock of the mountain. You couldn't see it just like that, but a dungeon was dug dip inside the mountain, making it a natural prison.

Arius didn't even look at me as we arrived. He didn't say anything and went straight inside. The guards at the gate looked at me with interrogating eyes.

"Welcome back Prince Damien," they told me.

I knew I couldn't just keep her in my arms, so I told the guards, "Find her some clothes and put her in the dungeon."

The guards took her and went on to do as I asked.

As I entered the castle, I was greeted by my mother.

"Hi, my son, how did it go?" she inquired.

It was a mess if you ask me. We sent out to steal an heirloom but winded up having a war and kidnapping a girl.

I looked at my mom, still beautiful after all those years. Vampires age very slowly and live for hundreds of years. She was only four hundred years old. I loved her dearly.

"It didn't go as we've planned. We were caught and had to put up a fight. And on top of that, we didn't find the heirloom."

She looked disappointed. "Oh, I see … are you hurt?"

I laughed at her question. I might be two hundred and twenty-seven years old, she still looked after me like a child.

"I'm fine mom, I'm not a kid anymore." I told her teasingly.

She pondered for a moment. "You will always be my child; however old you get."

I smiled at her, then she asked, "What were those guards carrying? I thought maybe you've found the heirloom and it was bigger than we thought, but since you've said you didn't find it, I guess it's something else."

I felt my heart racing in my chest as I frantically searched for something to answer. "It's a she-wolf. We couldn't find the heirloom, but surely she will be able to tell us about it."

I was patting myself on the back mentally to have thought of this explanation.

My mother's eyes widened. "You brought a she-wolf here? What if they try to get her back?"

I shrugged my shoulders. "It was the only way to gain more details about the heirloom."

My mother looked worried.

"Whom did you take? Where did you find her?"

I didn't really have the answer to her questions, I didn't even know her name. "We found her in the house." I simply answered, which was true.

My mother looked at me with a worried face.

"Damien, you need to talk to your father about this… He's not going to be pleased."

I knew damn well she was right. I really didn't want to face my father right now.

"I need to take a shower first. The stench of blood is still on my body."

I turned around and went to my room.

As I reached my room, which had an en-suite bathroom, I went straight for the shower I let the hot water run down my back, trying to relax, but all I could think of was her. I missed her smell, I wanted to hold her in my arms. What will she think when she wakes up all alone in the dungeon? Damn those thoughts made no sense. Why was I thinking about her like that? How could it be? Even if I tried to lie to myself, it was obvious that I cared about her.

I hit the wall with my fist in anger. What the hell is wrong with me? I'm a vampire and she's a werewolf. We are enemies. I have no right to care about her.

How could I have fallen so fast for her? I never fell for a vampire female. I've had a lot of girlfriends in my two hundred and twenty-seven years of existence, even a few mistresses here and there. But it was mostly for fun. Nothing serious. I've never felt such a strong pull to anyone before. I didn't even know her! The only logical explanation would be that she was my mate.

They say the mate bond between two vampires is strong. But I've never heard anything about werewolves and vampires being mates.

Whatever it was I was feeling, it could never happen. I had to forget about it. We were born enemies; it would have to stay that way. For generations, our ancestors fought. There's no way I could mate with a she-wolf. Damn I was so angry at myself for having those thoughts! All the more, I was a prince, the heir to the throne. I would find a nice vampire lady and that's it. No more thinking about her.

I got out of the shower, convinced I had managed to get those crazy ideas out of my head, and dressed properly. I put on a formal shirt with short sleeves and a black pant. With my loose hair, I think it gave a relaxed but still chic princely look.

A knock came on my door. I opened the door. A human slave was there. He bowed lowly.

"Welcome back my prince. Your father would like to speak with you right away."

Of course, he would, I thought. I guess my brother went right to him to report everything that had happened. I was not looking forward to this meeting. An angry vampire lord can be quite scary. What's more, he's way stronger than I am since vampires gain in strength as they become kings and queens.

I clenched my teeth at the thought of meeting with my father.

"Tell him I'm coming right away."

The slave bowed and went to deliver my message.

I knew I had to go see my father without delay. I closed my eyes and took a deep breath. The sooner I get this over with, the better it will be.

I made my way to my father's room. The slave was already waiting at the door to let me in. I could feel my father's anger surging through the door. He was not in a good mood, that was for sure.

As I entered the room, my brother exited. He didn't even look at me. He just stared right in front of him and got out.

I walked a few feet from my father. I could feel a sort of aura of anger around him. The air was charged with emotion. I was getting nervous. Everybody knows not to mess with the vampire lord.

The thing is, I never really got along with my father. Fighting with him was one of my hobbies. But the fact that he was already pissed at me before we even started to talk made this more dangerous.

I was better off not to piss him off too much...

He talked first, "is it true what I've heard? Not only did you not find the heirloom you were sent to get, but you've stopped your brother from killing a wolf and you even brought her back here?"

Straight to the point. I guess my brother did tell him everything. Oh well … saves me the trouble.

I had nothing to deny so I just confirmed what happened. "It is."

My father slammed his fist angrily at his desk. "How did I raise such a weak heir!"

I got angry and shouted back, "Valuing someone's life is not weak father!"

He looked at me with fury in his eyes. I stepped back unconsciously. If he were to attack me, I wouldn't be able to overpower him. No father in their right mind would kill their son but you never know.

"You dare to retort? You'd better have a good reason for bringing her here and not killing her or you will not see the day you take the throne. Do you have any idea what will happen if her pack were to come here to try to rescue her?"

I started to get nervous, but I was trying to hide it. My heartbeat was picking up the pace. I was sure my father could feel it, but I hoped he wouldn't make a big deal out of it.

What if he doesn't like my answer?

It was the only answer I had anyways, so I took my bravest tone.

"We were not finding the heirloom anywhere. She surely knows where it is. I will get the information out of her."

My father frowned. He looked annoyed but the answer seemed to satisfy him at least a little.

"You'd better get the information out of her," he said threateningly. "Remember that the future vampire lord cannot show weaknesses, my son … Now be gone! Before I change my mind."

I released the breath I didn't know I was holding, took a small bow and exited the room.

When I got out of the room, I saw my brother, arms crossed, just beside the door. He had a stern look on his face, eyes closed.

"So, is it really why you brought her here?"

Of course, he must have heard everything from outside the door.

My brother and I were quite different. We didn't get along very well, but I guess that's brotherly love.

We made our way to our rooms as we talked.

"Yes, of course, I brought her here to find the heirloom. Why else would I?"

Arius snorted.

"Yeah, well I don't buy it. Do as you please, just don't mess up. You'd better give Dad what he wants or else you know what's going to happen."

I knew very well what could happen if I were to displease our father. He would surely kill me if I didn't do as he liked. He had a cruel way of leading the throne and he expected his sons to do the same. He ruled people with fear. He didn't hesitate to execute people who displeased him. I was sure he wouldn't hesitate to punish his own sons. I would make sure he would be satisfied.

"Of course, I am aware of what would happen. I will not let that come about."

As I neared my room, a slave approached me.

55

"She is awake, my prince."

I froze for a second, my mouth agape, but then composed myself.

"Good, I will go see her."

My brother chuckled.

"You might fool the old man, but you're not fooling me. Have fun."

With that, he was out of my sight.

I watched my brother leave, wondering just what he meant by that. I didn't ponder for long, now on my way to see the she-wolf in the dungeon. My heart was racing, my head full of questions, not really knowing what to expect.

************ Kate's POV ************

I opened my eyes slowly. I was freezing and my mind was cloudy. I looked around and saw that I was in a cold room that looked like a prison cell. That's right! The vampires in my room! We fought and … and the first vampire. The last thing I remember is him, saying he was sorry.

God, I hated him so much for capturing me. Raged boiled inside me. I wasn't strong enough. How would I make a good Alpha? I needed to get stronger.

I looked around the room. The walls looked like they were made of stone. There was a small bed. There's no way I'm going to sleep in this. There was a window but way too small for anyone to even think about escaping this way.

The only door was at the end of the room, made of steel. A small window in the upper part of the door, with security bars in it, could let me talk with the guards... I guess. Like I wanted to talk to them anyway.

I shivered. From the looks of it, I would say this room was in the basement or something like that. It could explain why it feels so cold even though it was sunny and warm outside. I could feel drafts of air coming through the walls. The air felt humid, and it smelled almost like I was in a cave.

The dress I was wearing was too big for me and did no good in keeping me warm. How the hell did I get changed into this?

Oh right... I changed to my wolf during the fight... Which meant... They had seen me naked. In moments like these, I cursed my ability to change to my wolf form... I don't mind being naked when I change back, but not in front of my enemy.

Well, whatever they wanted from me, they're not getting it. I just need some time, a little time, and I'll find a way to get out of here. I'll show them what the daughter of the Alpha can do. I'll teach them not to mess with us.

When somebody comes, I'll just attack and run through the door. I don't know why I froze earlier, but I won't make that mistake again.

*********** Damien's POV ***********

When I got to the dungeon, she was sitting in a corner of the cell with her legs curled up. She was looking at the floor so I couldn't see her eyes. Her brown hair was coming down to the middle of her back. She had a loose dress on that was a little too large for her, so her shoulders and neck were naked. I guess it was the only available clothes the guards could find. God, I found her skin so irresistible. All I could think of, was how I would like to kiss that neck of hers. As I studied her, I realized my fangs had started to grow without me even thinking about it. I retracted them immediately.

I shook my head. What was wrong with me? I had to cast those thoughts away. That was not the reason I was here for.

As I entered the cell, she looked at me. I had to fight myself not to go to her. I stayed near the door, standing. I knew I couldn't resist my urges if I went too close to her.

She was scared, I could sense her fast heartbeat. I put on a stern face as much as I could and tried to hide all traces of emotions as I spoke to her, "What is your name?"

She looked at me with hatred in her eyes. Good, that's going to help me get those feelings out of the way.

She replied defiantly, "like I'm going to tell you."

So much fire in her, I liked a feisty woman. But again, I had to remind myself she was my prisoner.

"Fine, I guess I'll call you little wolf then. Tell me little wolf, where are you hiding your family heirloom?"

She looked at me with questioning eyes.

"I have no idea what you're talking about and even if I knew, I wouldn't tell you."

I snorted at her answer and answered coldly, "fine, we'll see how much time before you talk."

I observed her, watching in silence as she shivered. It was rather cold in the dungeon and that dress didn't cover enough skin to keep her warm.

Good, I thought to myself. That ought to make her talk faster. I turned around and left her cell.

I talked to the guard outside her cell.

"Do not leave her side. If she wants to talk, come and get me. See that she gets some food and water but nothing more."

The guard acknowledged my orders. I wouldn't want her to die before revealing the secrets she had.

Chapter 3 (Damien)

Interrogation

I went back to my room and tried to go about my business but couldn't concentrate. All I could think about was her. Her smooth skin that looked so soft. Her scent that smelled so sweet. Why couldn't I get her out of my mind? Why did fate mate me with a she-wolf? Couldn't I get a nice female vampire like everyone else? Knowing she was cold and alone in the dungeon was driving me crazy. But then again, I had to remind myself that it's not like she would allow me to give her company. I was her abductor; I was the enemy. It was better this way.

I was lost in my thoughts when someone knocked on my door. I opened the door and sure enough my brother was there. He looked at me from head to toe.

"What the hell happened to you?"

I looked at him with doubtful eyes.

"You look miserable."

I didn't really know what to answer. Did he suspect what I felt for her? I didn't intend to find out right now. Vampires and werewolves are enemies. It's not like anything is going to change anytime soon.

I shrugged my shoulders.

"Did you look at yourself in a mirror lately?"

My brother laughed at my question.

"I try not to. Broken mirrors bring bad luck."

I chuckled, then replied.

"Having a prisoner is not exactly my cup of tea."

"Huh, if you say so… By the way, I came here because Dad called a strategic meeting for our war on the werewolves."

The war... I was looking forward to it. That is, before I met her. Now, I wasn't so sure I wanted to go to war anymore. But I knew we didn't have a choice. The werewolves broke the peace treaty eighteen years ago. Since then, my father had been preparing our troops. We couldn't back down now.

Sadness returned at the thought of the war. I looked at my brother with empty eyes.

"Yeah, okay I'm coming..."

My brother shouted, "For crying out loud! What happened to you? Where's that fire of yours? You used to be all eager for this war to start. But now, I don't even recognize my own brother!"

What was I supposed to answer?

I couldn't tell him that I met my mate, that she was a wolf and that I didn't want to go to war anymore. Vampires and werewolves were not supposed to fall in love, it goes against nature.

I hid my emotions as much as I could.

"I don't know what you're talking about. You worry too much about me. Let's go to this meeting."

I didn't give him a chance to answer anything. I got out of my room and started walking to the meeting room, my brother following me.

We entered the meeting room. There were a lot of people. My mother, Drusilla, was there. She was the queen of vampires; her role was to council and assist my father as much as she could, she was my father's advisor on lots of things and he consulted her as needed.

Of course, my father Orpheus was there also. He was the vampire lord and was making all the decisions. The two of them, being the lord and queen, had elevated powers and strength compared to the other vampires.

Then there was my brother and I, the two princes. We also had elevated powers compared to the other vampires but less than our parents.

And then there was my aunt Lilith. She was my mother's sister and also was of royal blood. She was still powerful, even though she was not the queen. She was one of our strongest generals and seemed very invested in this war.

I remember that a few years ago, she was a completely different person. Something happened and changed her, but I never got to know what exactly. From that day on, she closed her feelings to everyone, even my mother didn't know what happened to her.

She started to focus on the war. She had a lot of intel on the wolves. No one knew where she was getting all that information, but she was one of our best assets.

A lot of vampires came to fear her, but I didn't. When I was younger, I loved playing with my aunt. She was always sweet and smiling with me. I still hold on to that feeling in my heart.

The meeting started. My father took the lead, he talked about our forces, our attack plans. His rambling went on and on, there was no end to it.

I wasn't really listening when all of a sudden, my brother hit me on the shoulder. "Damien!" my brother hissed.

I looked around and everyone was staring at me. "What?"

My father looked pissed; he cleared his throat.

"I said, did you get the confession from the prisoner about the heirloom?"

Oh that, I thought to myself.

"Not yet, I'll give her a day or two, she'll speak, I'm sure of it."

The werewolf's heirloom... We didn't know what it was exactly. We just knew it was something powerful, passed down from one generation to another. Our sorcerer said we would need it if we wanted to have the upper hand in the war.

My aunt Lilith squinted her eyes.

"I would like to see this prisoner. I'll get it out of her."

I didn't like her tone; I didn't want her to hurt my little wolf. But I couldn't say that here. I couldn't say "no" to her either. The best I could do was go with her in the cell when she goes.

"Of course, we shall go later today."

She seemed satisfied with my answer. The meeting finally came to an end.

A guard came in and dropped a plate in my cell before leaving. The food smelled good, I hadn't eaten all day and my stomach growled. Nothing assured me there was not poison or some sort of truth serum in that food. There was no way I was eating this. I'm not drinking either. Screw this. I'm not cooperating, even if it means I die.

Thinking back to earlier. I thought I had a plan. But when he came into the cell, I froze … again… What the hell is wrong with me? I heard my wolf call to me. She wanted me to go to him. But I told her to stop, she must be wrong. That man kidnapped me. He was the enemy. He was a vampire, for god's sake! Why was I so attracted to him?

If I can't beat him, then I'll find another way. If I must, I will let myself die here. Maybe if I'm lucky, the pack will come and find me soon. Even better, when someone else comes into the cell, if it's not him, then surely, I'll be able to attack.

Never in my life have I felt so desperate. Captured
by my worst enemies, stuck in a cold cell. And
even worse, my wolf calling me to go to the one
who captured me. Tears dripped down my cheeks
in silence.

************ Damien's POV ************

We all gathered at the table to eat supper in the
grand hall. The floor was tiled with black and
white marble. Columns coming up from the floor
to the ceiling supported elaborated arches on the
ceiling. Crystal chandeliers sparked their light
upon the room and musicians played a soft music.

The best blood was poured into our glasses and
an exquisite banquet was served. It was a feast in
prevision for the upcoming war. We all ate, talked
and laughed, having a good time together,
forgetting for a short amount of time everything
that needed to be done.

After supper, it was decided my aunt and I would
go see the she-wolf. I brought a warm blanket
with me. I met Lilith in front of the cell. She
looked at the blanket in my hand and raised an

eyebrow. "We wouldn't want her to freeze to death." I explained.

She shrugged her shoulders and entered the cell.

The she-wolf was still at the same spot as earlier, curled up on herself, crying and shaking. She raised her head when we entered. My aunt had a startled look on her face for a moment when she saw her but then composed herself.

The she-wolf looked at my aunt, mouth agape. She stood up; she was at least two heads smaller than me. She looked like a fragile flower to me, but I knew she was strong, she had that fiery energy that I liked so much.

Pointing to my aunt, the she-wolf said, "I know you … who are you?"

Lilith answered with a cold stare, "You must be mistaken. This is the first time we have met."

But the she-wolf insisted, "no! I've smelled your scent before. I know we've met."

I didn't know why but I could see anger boiling down inside my aunt. She raised her hands and used her telekinetic powers on the she-wolf, pinning her to the wall.

She snapped at her, "and *I*, told you we just met. Don't contradict me. And learn when you should keep your mouth shut, beast."

The she-wolf's feet didn't touch the ground anymore. She was floating in the air, held by my aunt's powers.

I could see Lilith was tightening her grip on the she-wolf, suffocating her. The she-wolf was trying to make my aunt release her, trying to undo her neck from my aunt's invisible grasp with her hands. I could see her eyes panicking as she couldn't breathe anymore.

I couldn't let Lilith hurt my little wolf. I shouted at her, "enough!"

I sent a small wave of energy in the direction of my aunt, just enough to make her release her grasp. The she-wolf fell back on the ground as my aunt released her, taking a deep breath of air.

"Why did you do that?" Lilith asked me, furious, rubbing her wrists.

"You were going to kill her!"

"What does it matter to you?" she asked with a daunting look.

"I didn't bring her here to have her killed. And she won't talk much if she's dead," I answered with a defying look. My aunt seemed to ponder a little and then smirked a little.

"Humph, as I suspected... I'll let you deal with the prisoner, get the information out of her. But just so you know, you should have known better than to kidnap the daughter of the Alpha. He's going to be pissed."

With that said, my aunt left without turning back.

"... The daughter of the Alpha?" I repeated. I was alone with the she-wolf. She was looking at me with wide eyes, still on the floor where she fell.

"Yes, I am... I thought you knew. I thought that's why you took me." She watched me calmly, waiting for an answer.

I was astounded. How could my aunt know about that? It made no sense.

"... How did she know about you?"

The she-wolf shrugged her shoulder. "I know I've seen her before. I just don't remember where."

She was trying to remember where she'd seen my aunt. She was frowning while thinking and that made her look so cute. I had a hard time resisting the urge to laugh. I just wanted to take her into my arms and hug her, make sure she was not hurt anywhere. But I had to remind myself what I was supposed to do.

Suddenly she asked, as if just realizing, "You didn't know I was the Alpha's daughter. Then why did you take me?" pulling me out of my thoughts.

She was looking at me with a playful look that made her seem even prettier to me. It was a playful defiant kind of look, as if she was gauging me.

I smiled, embarrassed. "I really didn't know you were the Alpha's daughter. We were just looking for the heirloom. If you could just tell me where it is, I could let you go."

She looked at the floor.

"I already told you, I don't know what you're talking about."

I guess she wasn't ready to talk yet. Or maybe she was telling the truth? Maybe she really didn't know about it. I couldn't make my mind on which one it was.

"Okay little wolf. I guess it's time for me to say goodnight."

I threw her the blanket. She caught it and looked at me, surprised.

"I wouldn't want you to freeze to death tonight."

I started going back to the door when I heard, "Kate... My name is Kate... I never did tell you my name."

I turned around to see her looking at me with her beautiful hazel eyes.

I smiled at her. "Nice to meet you, Miss Kate. I'm Damien."

She smiled back at me, and it melted my heart. I could get used to seeing that smile. I got out of the cell and went back to my room.

*********** Kate's POV ***********

So … his name is Damien. Why did I tell him my name? Why did I smile at him. I wanted to be strong. To hold my ground.

He gave me a blanket. I needed this so much! Well, it's not like I would need it if I wasn't imprisoned in that damned cell! But still, he didn't have to do this. And I appreciate it.

The blanket is warm and soft. His scent is impregnated on it, and I can't seem to stop smelling it. And now, my wolf won't stop saying it clearly in my mind: mate. I keep telling her she's wrong. There's no way he can be my mate. He's a vampire! I need to find a strong wolf to lead the pack with me. But she won't listen to me.

I wrap myself in the blanket as I drift in my thoughts. He didn't know I was the Alpha's daughter. I was sure it was the reason they took me. He keeps talking about an heirloom. I have absolutely no idea what he means.

And who was that other vampire? The woman, I swear I know her! Why can't I remember her? I remember her scent. That's for sure. We werewolves have very advanced sense of smell and when we smell someone, we're almost sure to remember their scent.

Not finding an answer to my questions, the weight of everything that had happened today fell on my shoulders. Combined with the fact I had eaten nothing, I felt rather sleepy. I curled myself on the floor, wrapped in the blanket Damien's brought me. Taking one last breath of his scent, I let myself drift to sleep.

Chapter 4 (Damien)

Getting to know each other

I repeated to myself, "Kate." What a beautiful name. I finally had a name to put on her face. I couldn't keep denying it to myself. She was my mate. There was no way for me to ignore it. I didn't know if she felt the same way and there was no way for me to find out. I mean I did kidnap her, it would be normal for her to resent me. It's not like I could just walk in there and ask her if she felt she was my mate. So, I just stayed there, lying on my bed, staring at the ceiling and remembering her sweet smile over and over again. I couldn't talk to anyone about this. I would have to keep it to myself and try to hide it as much as I could.

I tried to fall asleep, but every time, my thoughts drifted back to Kate. Was she okay by herself in the dungeon? Was she still cold or was the blanket I gave her enough to keep her warm? The guards have told me she didn't eat a single thing since she got here. I didn't want her to starve to death. Would someone hurt her in her cell? Technically, anyone, my brother, my aunt or even my father had the right to go in her cell and do whatever they like to her without me knowing. I tossed and turned all night, I couldn't bear to be away from her, not knowing if she was safe.

Soon, the first rays of the sun showed themselves. I hadn't slept the whole night. One thing was clear to me; I couldn't keep up like that. I had to know she was well, or else I wouldn't be able to rest. My body ached from the fatigue; my head was about to explode.

I went to take a hot shower, letting the hot water run on my back. I put on a pair of jeans and a simple black V-neck. Then, before even eating breakfast, I made my way to the dungeon.

The guards looked surprised to see me.

"My prince! You are up early."

I looked at them with stern eyes.

"The prisoner is to stay in my room until further notice."

They had a bewildered look on their face, but they wouldn't dare to question the heir to the throne's decision.

"Yes, your majesty, we will go get her right away."

I stopped them right before they could go.

"No, I will go get her myself."

I left them with their mouths agape and entered Kate's cell.

When I entered the cell, she was sleeping in a corner on the floor, with the blanket I gave her. At least it kept her warm enough to be able to sleep. Sleeping like that, she looked like an angel. I didn't want to wake her up, but I was eager to get her out of here. I also wanted to make sure to get some food into her body.

I walked to her, but she didn't wake up. I got down to her level and replaced a fallen strand of her hair. I gently stroked her cheek with my hand and sure enough, her skin was as smooth as I imagined. I softly called her name, "Kate, wake up."

She opened her eyes slowly but then startled and got back. When she saw it was me, she relaxed.

"Oh, it's you Damien! You scared me."

I smiled at the fact that she was relieved it was me. That meant at least she wasn't afraid of me, or that she trusted me.

"Whom did you think it was?"

She thought before answering.

"Well, another vampire, like the one who was with you the other night, or anyone who would want to hurt me."

The vampire that was with me the other night, she meant my brother. I could totally understand her, we did attack her when we were in her room. Also, being abducted and kept in a cell in the dungeon can be quite stressful. Even more of a reason to get her out of here and into a proper room where she'll be safe, my room.

"Yes, you mean my brother. He was there with me the other night. Don't worry, I will make sure you are safe. I know being kept prisoner is not the best. But from now on, you will be staying in the safest place you can be in this castle. Somewhere where you won't be cold, and you'll be treated right."

She looked unsure.

"And may I ask where that is?"

I smiled. "My room."

She had a bewildered look on her face as her mouth went agape. I gave her my hand and asked, with a smirk on my face.

"Coming?"

She looked at my hand with doubtful eyes for a few seconds but decided to take it. I felt electricity passing through our hands as she grabbed my hand. Her skin was so warm and soft. I never wanted to let go of her hand. I was happy she decided to come, I didn't think she would accept. I guess staying in my room must be better than staying in the dungeon.

I led her to my room, which was on the fourth floor of the castle. As I opened the door, she scanned the room with her eyes. There was a window at the far end of the room with a desk. In one of the corners was a small table with two chairs. That's where I'd receive guests on some occasions. Two small couches occupied the other corner. Then stood my bed, filled with cushions and pillows. The wall beside my bed was composed of two closets filled with clothes. Finally, the en-suited bathroom, complete with a shower and a bath.

Kate looked like she was impressed. "Is this really where I'll be staying?"

I smiled. I could understand her reaction.

"Yes, you will be staying with me in my room. This is the safest place you can be in the castle. No one can harm you in here, I'll be there to protect you."

She looked around and realized out loud, "There's only one bed."

I laughed at her remark. "Don't worry, I'll stay on my side."

I had asked one of my closets to be filled with women's clothing this morning before going to the dungeon. That way, she could find something to wear better than the dress she currently had. I opened the closet to show it to her.

"You can choose whatever you would like to wear, I've made them available for you."

She looked at me in disbelief. "Why would you do all of this for me? I mean, first you abduct me and then you treat me like a princess?"

I looked at her, I understood what she meant. I couldn't tell her that for the little time I've known her, she found a way to steal my heart without even trying.

I just wanted to make her feel better while she was here, get the information I needed from her, and then let her go so she could be free.

I looked at her, she was waiting for an answer.

"I just wanted you to be more comfortable than in the dungeon. At least you will not be cold, and you will be safe. I told you already, I do not wish to harm you. I just need some information from you and then you'll be free."

She looked at me uneasy.

"I've already told you, I don't know what heirloom you are talking about."

I looked in her hazel eyes, she looked like she was telling the truth. Which was kind of a problem since my father was waiting for me to get the heirloom of the wolves in order to win the war.

I wanted to reassure her.

"It's okay, why don't you go take a shower and then we'll figure this out while eating breakfast."

She still looked unsure. "… You're not going to drink my blood, are you?"

I laughed at her question. "Is this what you think we vampires do? Drink blood from everyone all the time?"

She had this guilty look on her face. "Well, it's not every day that I get to chat with a vampire," she explained.

She was right, I guess her picture of vampires was as wrong as our picture of werewolves.

"Don't worry, I eat food too and I drink other stuff than blood too. All the more reason for us to chat after your shower."

She seemed happy with my answer, since she smiled. Her smile was so pretty, it took my breath away. I wanted to see that smile of hers more often so I could cherish it in as many memories as possible.

She went in the closet, picked out an outfit and went to take a shower. I couldn't believe how lucky I was she decided to trust me. I mean, would you really trust the person who abducted you?

As I heard the water running in the shower, all I could think about was that she was naked in the bathroom. I was trying to imagine what she looked like, the curves of her body, her smooth skin and her sweet smell. How I wish I could go see, but I would never do that.

Instead, I ordered breakfast from one of the slaves of the castle and instructed him to bring the breakfast to my room.

*********** Kate's POV ***********

The hot water of the shower felt like a blessing. I feel like it's been such a long time since I showered. This felt great! Relaxing, I pondered on everything that just happened. I didn't know why he decided to get me out of that cell, but I couldn't be happier. I still didn't know if I could trust him fully. Although my wolf was screaming at me to trust him, she was repeating the same thing over again: mate.

It was kind of a weird feeling. Being attracted to the guy that's supposed to be my enemy. I really didn't know what to expect when he talked about eating breakfast... I thought vampires only drank blood all the time. I guess I don't know a lot about vampires after all. It makes me curious to learn more about him.

I'm really happy that I'm getting to stay in his room instead of the cell. I'll get to sleep in an actual comfortable bed! I can't believe how much clothes there was for me to choose what I wanted to wear. Why would he have all those women's clothes in his closet? Does he have a girlfriend? No, I smelled no scent other than his in his room. Why am I even wondering if he has a girlfriend? God I can't keep these thoughts under control!

I guess that's why I chose a cute summer dress to wear. I smiled at myself. I know I'll look cute in it. I'm eager to see his reaction when I come out of the shower with that dress. Having breakfast will be nice too, since I had not eaten at all yesterday. This is turning out to be more fun than expected, I thought to myself as I finished showering myself and prepared to get out.

*********** Damien's POV ************

As I waited for Kate to come out of the shower, I tried to think of what the next steps would be. I needed to find the heirloom. But again, there was this war coming up and I didn't want to go to war anymore. I needed a way to prevent this war from happening, even if it was already starting.

A knock came at the door. I opened and found a slave bringing me the breakfast I ordered. I took the food from him and closed the door. I noticed the shower wasn't running anymore, which meant that Kate would come out soon. I set up the food on the table, waiting for her to exit of the bathroom.

A few seconds later, Kate came out of the bathroom. My jaw dropped when I saw her. She was wearing a beautiful red summer dress that was hugging her curves just enough before flowing down. Her still wet hair was up in a loose bun. She was breathtaking. She saw me looking at her and smirked when she saw the face I was making.

Embarrassed, I passed my hand through my hair as I smiled at her. "You look beautiful."

She grinned. "Thanks."

Her eyes widened as she saw all the food on the table.

"I didn't know what you liked so I ordered a little bit of everything," I explained.

She laughed and sat at the table. "Looks like I can have whatever I could think of!"

I sat in front of her, and we started to eat.

As we ate, we talked about a lot of things. Kate had a lot of questions about vampires. It appears that werewolves thought we were soulless blood sucking monsters that attacked every living thing restlessly.

Also, that we didn't eat or drink anything other than blood and would die if we went in the sunlight. Which was not true since we were both sitting under the sunlight right now and I was feeling perfectly fine.

Hearing these things, no wonder they hated us. Maybe if we took some time to know each other, there could be a lasting peace between our kinds.

As for myself, I asked Kate all the questions I had about werewolves. Like for instance, I thought they only changed into their wolves' form at full moon, which was not true.

Or that they attacked everyone on sight when they changed, which was also not true.

I learned that the wolf's pack is like a big family that protects each other, which I find is really nice. I wished vampire's families were like that.

By the time we finished eating, we were done with all our questions. Now it was time to get to the real topic, the heirloom.

Kate was enjoying her coffee. I looked her in the eyes. Her hazel eyes bewitched me. I could easily get lost in them. My eyes fell on her luscious lips. They were so inviting, I had to remember for a moment what I wanted to talk about.

"So tell me Kate, you say you don't know anything about an heirloom?"

"No … but maybe you could describe it to me, and I could see if it reminds me of anything."

I knew she was being honest. I could feel it. I couldn't perceive any sign she was lying like an increase of her heartbeat. She was looking me straight in the eyes, no twitching.

"Well, we don't really know what it looks like, but Lilith told us this family heirloom holds great power and is passed from generation to generation through the alpha's family."

Kate's eyes widened. "Lilith? Who is that?"

I forgot she didn't know her name. "She was the vampire with me yesterday when we came to see you in the dungeon."

She seemed to remember. "Oh yes! The one that I've seen before!"

Just now, I could see her eyes light up as she got excited. She was so pretty it made me smile. "Right, how can you be so sure you've met her before?"

Kate smiled at me. "We werewolves have a very advanced sense of smell. We remember very well the scent of the people we meet."

I laughed a little. "Huh, so what do I smell like?"

Kate giggled and thought for a second before answering.

"Hum, you smell a little like honey mixed with musk."

I smirked and then teased her a little. "I guess I must smell good then."

She blushed at my comment. I just hoped she didn't ask how she smelled. Because to me, she smelled like heaven.

Luckily, she didn't ask about it.

"As I've told you, I am the oldest daughter of the Alpha. And I am not aware of any family heirloom being passed down by our family. Why do you guys want it so bad anyways?"

My eyes darkened and my heart sank at her question.

"Well... Our sorcerer told us we would need its power in order to win the war," I said with pain in my voice.

Kate seemed sad. "Oh... I see."

She was looking down at the floor, avoiding my eyes.

"Damn that war!" I said angrily. "Why did you have to break the treaty?"

She looked at me with widened eyes and said with an accusing tone. "We didn't! You are the ones who trespassed in our territory! You broke the treaty."

It hit me. She thought we just started the war this week when we went to her house!

I looked at her.

"Didn't you not know? Eighteen years ago, werewolves stole a particularly important book from the vampires. A book that holds all our history and our secrets. That's what broke the treaty, not us breaking your territory."

Kate stopped talking and thought for a moment.

"Listen Damien, I've never heard of any vampire book or anything like that. All that I know is that you guys came to my house and abducted me."

I couldn't believe what I was hearing. Was it true? Was the book stolen by werewolves? Or was it maybe just a reason for the vampire lord to wage war?

I knew my father hated werewolves, as his father was killed by one, years ago. Would he go that far as to fake a robbery to have a reason to go to war?

From the wolf's point of view, we were the bad guys from one end to the other. But from our standpoint, they were the bad guys. Something smelled fishy and I didn't like it.

I wanted to talk with her about this more, but someone knocked on my door.

Kate looked at me worried, her heartbeat increasing. I gave her a reassuring look and sure enough, I could hear her heartbeat slow back down to its normal speed.

I opened the door to see my brother come in. He looked at Kate and then started with a smirk on his face. "Well, well. It seems that what I've heard was true. You decided to keep her into your room, have you?"

He was annoying me. "This is none of your business Arius." I snapped at him.

My brother ignored me. "Oh, but it is. Father asked me to bring her to the sorcerer."

Kate gasped and stepped back a little.

I blocked my brother's way and told him with anger, "you will not lay a finger on her."

My brother snickered, "just as I thought, you care about her. Maybe I should tell Father that my older brother has lost his mind and prefers to protect a beast than to obey his lord?"

I hated his guts! He knew I didn't have a choice in this matter, or I risked death.

What disgusted me even more, was how he called her. "She's not a beast!" I shouted.

I needed to take back control of myself as I was feeling I was about to lose it.

"Okay, okay," my brother said. "There's no need to get so agitated," he added with a smirk. He knew he hit a sensitive cord.

I asked, "What does he want with her anyways?"

Arius shrugged his shoulders. "I don't know, he was mumbling something about the heirloom and tests he wanted to do on her... Anyways, I need to bring her to the sorcerer right away."

I stopped my brother again. "It's okay, I'll bring her to the sorcerer myself."

He shrugged his shoulders and spoke teasingly, "as you wish, lover boy."

And with that, he turned away and got out of my room, still laughing. I guess it was *that* obvious... Still, I didn't expect him to accept that easily the fact that I loved her.

I turned to Kate, to see her shaking, pale as ever. I went to her and took her in my arms. She looked up at me.

"What is he going to do with me?"

I wished I knew. "I don't know, but I will not let him harm you, okay?"

Tears began dripping down her beautiful face. I hugged her against my chest, wiping away each tear with my hand. The warmth of her body felt so good against me. She put her arms around my back, hugging me, and slowly stopped crying.

I wished for this moment to last forever. I could feel her heartbeat against my chest and her warm breath on my neck. The bare skin of her neck and shoulders were so tempting. How I wished I could taste her! I craved her so much it was hurting me.

I wanted more of this, I wanted her all. We stayed like that, in each other's arms for a moment before breaking the embrace.

I cupped her face with my hand.

"Listen Kate, I really wish I didn't have to bring you to the sorcerer. But I can't disobey my father on this."

Kate raised her face, looking at me with pleading eyes.

"Why can't you?"

This would probably shock her, but it was the truth.

"Because he would surely have me killed if I did."

She gaped at my words, looking horrified.

To anyone, this would sound astounding. But my father was known for his cruelty.

"My father keeps people in fear. He wouldn't hesitate to sacrifice his own children to show the people what the cost of disobeying is."

I could read sadness in Kate's eyes. I squeezed her hands as I spoke.

"I will not let them hurt you. I will be there for you, I promise."

Her smile reappeared on her face, that smile that lightens my heart every time I see it.

Chapter 5 (Damien)

The Sorcerer

How I wished that I could keep her in my arms forever. I wished I didn't have to bring her to the sorcerer. But it was time to go.

Kate looked up at me as I asked her, "Ready?" She nodded, and I could see determination in her eyes. She was strong and courageous, ready to face whatever awaited her. I liked that part of her so much. I tried to shove back all the fears I had in my mind and look as strong as her.

Together, we exited my room. I couldn't hold her hand, it would look strange. I tried not to walk too fast and made sure Kate stayed close to me. You never know what kind of vampire you can meet in these corridors. Some of them could very well try to attack Kate if they saw her.

We swiftly made our way to the sorcerer's room, which was on the same floor as my room.

We arrived at Elwin's laboratory. He was our sorcerer. He was a weird looking vampire. Not very tall, thin, his back a little curved from all those hours staying bent over his work. He was an old vampire and it started to show. I didn't know his exact age, but he was the lord's sorcerer even before my father took the throne. Gray hair started to show through his crow black hair. He kept them short at it was more practical for him this way, they wouldn't get in his face while working. Some of his fingers were crooked after years of repetitive tasks and he kept his fingernails sharp for dissecting.

His laboratory was cluttered with stuff everywhere, as usual. You could see dead animals in liquid filled jars. Some dead skulls lying here and there. All kinds of vials that only he knew what was inside. Books and cluster of dust were filling his shelves. A strange smell always seemed to linger in the air. Really, this room was the only

one that looked like that in the whole castle …
luckily!

Elwin looked up at us when we entered the room.
He bowed before me. "My prince, I was expecting
your brother. How nice of you to greet me with
your presence."

I looked at him; overall, he was not a bad guy. But
I didn't like the fact he wanted to do experiments
on Kate. I kept her by my side. I could tell she was
scared; I could feel her heartbeat rise. I squeezed
her hand, reminding her I wouldn't let her be
harmed, then released it. I couldn't afford for
anyone see me holding hands with her.

I looked at Elwin.

"What do you want with the girl?"

He grinned at my question and came closer,
studying Kate's face. He seemed lost in his
thoughts.

"Hum… I only want to do some tests to her,
nothing big, maybe a blood test also."

This didn't answer my question, I was getting quite annoyed at him. I raised my voice and ordered with authority.

"You are not to harm her in any way."

Elwin looked at me puzzled. I was a prince, and the heir to the throne. I knew he couldn't go against my order unless my father said otherwise. I sure hoped this matter wouldn't escalate up to my father. I would be pretty helpless against him.

But it didn't look like it would be a problem, as Elwin smiled and answered, "your wish is my order my prince. I shall be gentle with the prisoner."

He took Kate by the hand and proceeded to take her in one of his adjoining rooms. She was so nervous she was shaking a little. There was nothing I could do to ease her fear. I felt so helpless!

I started to follow, but Elwin turned back and said apologetically, "I'm sorry my prince but I'm going to have to ask you to wait here. Those experiments need to be done in the upmost silence with precision. No one can be present with me in the room except the experiment itself."

I hated the fact he talked about her like she was an object. I looked at him and replied threateningly, "Very well, but if I hear just a hint of a cry of pain, I'll come in and stop whatever you're doing. Am I clear?"

Elwin nodded and made his way to the room with Kate. Before Elwin closed the door, Kate turned to look at me. The fire in her eyes was replaced by fear. I watched, powerless, as the door closed.

It was incredibly hard to watch the woman I loved being taken away to have whatever experiments done on her. I was scared and angry at the same time. The only thing preventing me from grabbing her from Elwin's clutches was the fact that my father was way too powerful and would probably kill me if I interfered.

*********** Kate's POV ************

I was so scared. Just as I thought maybe things weren't so bad this morning, as I was finally getting to enjoy myself a little... I knew it was bad news when I heard Damien's brother talk about a sorcerer.

At least, Damien was with me. But he couldn't follow me in here. And now, I was all alone on this cold examination table. I felt my heart pounding in my chest like it was about to come out. I swallowed hard and tried to take a deep breath.

I looked around. I was in a sterilized and empty room. I knew it wouldn't be empty for a long time. The sorcerer said he wouldn't take long, he only needed to fetch some stuff for the experiment.

I looked around the room, there was no exit possible. On one side, there was the door where Elwin disappeared to get his stuff. This was not a good option. And on the other side was Damien. How I wished I could run back to him. It was no use. I knew he had no choice in the matter. It was his father's orders, the vampire lord. He couldn't go against it; it was useless to try to run away from this.

The only thing I could do was to stay strong and endure this moment. In the end, Damien did ask the sorcerer not to hurt me, right? So, whatever he was going to do, it shouldn't be too bad, right? And after that is over, Damien is going to get me and bring me back to his room. He said he would protect me. That I could stay with him so no one could harm me. I believe him, I know he was sincere when he said that.

I was lost in my thoughts when I heard a noise coming from the other room. I could hear metal instruments clicking together. Fear started to creep on me again as I realized that Elwin was coming back with his tools. I reminded myself that I needed to be strong. This was only a short moment to pass, it would soon be over, I told myself.

*********** Damien's POV ***********

She's been with Elwin for a few hours now. How much time do those experiments last? I was restless, waiting for her to come out of that room. I made sure to listen carefully for any signs she was in trouble. I could sense she was alive and scared.

She was my mate, I knew it, I felt it through all of my being. But I didn't know if she felt it too. I didn't really know how it worked either when it was a werewolf and a vampire together. I didn't even know if there's ever been a case of a werewolf and vampire mate.

All I knew was, for vampires, when they find their mates, as the relation grows between them, so does their bonds. It can get strong enough that sometimes, the mates can read each other's minds and communicate without speaking. But right now, we didn't have that kind of bond. She didn't know how I felt, we didn't even kiss or anything. So of course, I couldn't know what was happening to her right now, much less communicate with her.

All I could do was wait for her to come out of that room. That wait was killing me! I was a mess. Walking nervously from one end of the room to the other. Trying to take a seat but standing up at the first sound I hear. I swear if she didn't come out soon, I wouldn't be able to hold myself much longer.

I don't really know how much time passed but finally, the door opened, and Elwin walked out of it with a cart of tools and tubes. He looked at me and said casually.

"I'm done now, you can go and pick her up, I think she is too weak to walk right now."

Wait what? What did this mean? He was not supposed to hurt her! I felt anger boil through my veins as I walked towards him, saying in a low voice, "You weren't supposed to hurt her."

Elwin swallowed, fear and nervousness taking a hold of him, making him take a few steps back. He stuttered nervously, "m ... my prince ... please... I, I didn't hurt her. Please believe me. I only did experiments... You can ask her yourself."

I pondered. "You are right, I will ask her myself. And if she says you hurt her in any way, I'll be back. Understood?"

Elwin nodded his head nervously and went away as fast as he could with his cart.

I entered the room and saw Kate, my precious Kate, lying down on a table. Her beautiful dress had been cut and I could see little red dots and holes in her skin where Elwin must have plugged tubes or drawn blood from her.

Why did I let him do this to her? Surely, I could have thought of another solution. I felt guilty for what she had to live through. Not only was she abducted by her enemy, now she's had experiments done on her. She must have been so frightened. And I wasn't there to protect my mate. I let him do all of that to her, without doing anything to help her. I must be the worst mate ever.

Her skin was all pale, she looked so weak. I walked to her, caressing her arm carefully. Her body felt cold, she was alive, but looked so frail right now. She needed to heat up, and it's not like I could help her on that part. We vampires naturally have a lower body temperature. I should bring her in my bed, under the covers, she should be fine there. I carefully picked her up like she could break apart in my arms.

Her hand feebly grabbed my shirt, she half-opened her eyes and looked at me. She smiled as she only said, "Damien," with a small voice, before letting go of my shirt and closing her eyes again. Her, saying my name, made my heart flutter. But at the same time, I was so angry at myself for the state she was in. I hurried back to my room, holding my little wolf in my arms.

As I entered my room, I cautiously rested her on my bed. I went to the closet and picked a comfortable pajama for her, one that would also keep her warm. I didn't know if she would be okay with me changing her, but she was unconscious and needed to warm up, so I figured it was the correct thing to do.

I got her out of the dress, too worried about her state to even think about looking at her body, and swiftly got her into the pajamas. I got her in bed, under the sheets. I touched her forehead and sure enough, she was getting warmer, which was a good sign. Her breathing was getting regular. I sat on the bed, watching her sleep, keeping an eye on her. It wasn't nightfall already, but I didn't want to leave her alone. I finally decided to change myself into my boxers and lay by her side in the bed.

There she was, my mate, resting just a few inches away from me. I knew she was getting better; she was just resting; I could feel her body now warm.

Would it ever be possible for us to be together? Would she ever love me? I mean, I think she trusted me, which is a start. What am I to her? Does she despise me for taking her away from her home? Did she feel the mate bond or was I the only one feeling it? I had so many questions on my mind, so many questions that I couldn't possibly dare to ask if she was awake...

As soon as I get the information I need to please my father, I will let her go. That will be the best. But tonight, I was with her. I moved closer to her, making sure not to wake her up, and put my arm around her waist. I buried my face in the crook of her neck. Her skin was so soft, and her body was so warm compared to mine. She smelled like a delicate flower, and I held her gently, making sure not to break her. Being this close to her made my heart beat strong. Lying in bed, with my mate in my arms, knowing she would be safe tonight, exhausted from not sleeping the night before, I let myself fall to slumber in this paradise.

Chapter 6 (Kate)

Jealousy

I woke up to a familiar scent. I knew even without opening my eyes who it was, it was the sweet scent of Damien, this scent I couldn't resist. I opened my eyes and realized I was cuddled up in his arms. I smiled at that thought. My wolf was happy, wagging her tail. All she kept saying in my head was, "mate." I never imagined my mate would be a vampire.

Two days ago, when I saw him in my room in my parents' house, I thought it was fear that was making my heart beat fast. I fought with myself, told my wolf she was wrong, that he couldn't possibly be my mate. I tried to resist, tried to look strong. I was a wolf, the Alpha's daughter, he was a vampire, we were enemies. I had to stay strong so I could go back to my family. I needed a strong wolf, to lead the pack with me one day.

I tried so hard to fight this... But I couldn't keep lying to myself, he was my mate, whether I liked it or not. Yesterday, when he came to take me out of the cell to stay in his room, I knew I couldn't keep resisting. The mate bond was pulling me so strongly. My wolf wanted me to stay with him.

He was treating me like a princess. He was so sweet, thinking about my well-being. I had such a great time at breakfast. I got to know him better. I really felt protected with him. I could see it in his eyes; he wouldn't let anyone hurt me.

Yesterday, that's when I decided to stop fighting with my wolf. I didn't know it was possible for a vampire and a werewolf to be mates. The moon goddess sure liked to mess with me. I couldn't lie to myself and I couldn't fight my wolf. There was no denying he was my mate.

The way he made my heart flutter just by being in the room with me. The way I missed him when he was gone. The way his touch sends sparks to my body and the way his scent is driving me crazy.

And right now, the way I feel like I'm whole, with his cool body against mine. Not too cold that it's unpleasant. Just a little cool, refreshing. Like a refreshing breeze on a hot summer night.

I noticed he wasn't wearing a shirt, letting me see his sculpted chest and muscled arms. I thought he looked so perfect. I noticed he had a few tattoos on his chest and right arm. I guess I never noticed as he usually wears a shirt over it. I think the tattoos only increased his sexiness.

Instinctively, I approached his neck and took a deep breath of his scent. This scent of honey and musk was driving me insane. I wanted to wrap myself in it. Without thinking, I rubbed my cheek against his chest, rubbing my scent all over him, a low purr coming out of my chest. It was my wolf, she wanted to let everyone know he was hers, she wanted to mark him.

Although usually males mark females, it could also happen the other way around. Right now, my wolf wanted to make sure everybody knew he was ours. My teeth were grazing at his skin, at the spot where the neck meets the shoulder. That's usually where we mark our mates. But I knew I couldn't do it just like that. I resisted the urge to grow my canines to mark him.

I was lost in my thoughts when I heard a low laugh. I froze and blushed when I realized he was awake. I looked up, my eyes meeting his. He had a smirk on his face.

"Morning little wolf. Looks like you're feeling better." He had a teasing look on his face.

I'm pretty sure I was as red as a beet. I was so sure he was asleep; he wasn't supposed to see that. Embarrassed, the only thing I could do was smile. "You took good care of me, as you promised."

He chuckled, I guess he enjoyed having me close to him because he started to run his hands down my back, sending shivers down my spine. I closed my eyes for a second, enjoying the feeling he was giving me. A small moan escaped my lips. I wasn't really sure what was happening, but I was liking it.

Damien seemed to enjoy himself too as he had a sexy smirk on his face, his eyes full of desire. I whispered his name as I looked at him, my eyes full of lust. Damien brought his mouth close to my neck, and for a moment I could feel his teeth graze on my skin.

I thought maybe he would bite me. I've never been bitten by a vampire before but right now I didn't care one bit. But instead, he seemed to fight with himself and got a little further from me. I didn't really understand what was going on.

He spoke softly, "I'm sorry… I shouldn't."

I was disappointed. My wolf was not happy about this, she yearned for more, all of me wanted more, but this was happening all too soon. Whatever was happening anyway? I wasn't sure what to think of it either.

"Okay, let's just lie down a little bit more then; I like being in your arms."

He smiled at my reply and came back closer to hug me. "Yes, I like that too."

I was enjoying the moment in his arms when suddenly, I had flashbacks of yesterday, my dress being cut by the crazy sorcerer. When I looked at myself, I realized I was not in my dress anymore. I was in pajamas and I didn't remember changing myself.

I looked at Damien. "Did you change my clothes?"

He froze for a second at my question.

"You were cold and unconscious. I needed to get you warm or you could have died."

I could feel he was embarrassed, but he was telling the truth. I couldn't be mad at him for saving me, right?

"Thanks for saving me."

Damien smiled, "I told you I would keep you safe."

Being this close to him made my heart beat fast. His scent was intoxicating. I wished I could stay in his arms always. I looked at his eyes and noticed they were not red like when he was at my house. They were gray now, making his gaze look mysterious. I had never seen such beautiful eyes. When I looked into his eyes, it was as though I was looking for the first time at the sea.

I had wanted to ask him about his eye color. I didn't get the chance to do so before, so now was my chance to ask.

"Your eyes, the other day at my house, they were red. How are they gray now?"

He chuckled. "Our eyes only turn red if we are attacked or if we crave blood."

Huh I guess it made sense, I thought to myself as I nodded. My stomach grumbled; Damien laughed.

"Why don't you go get dressed and I'll order us breakfast?"

I laughed. "That sounds like a good idea."

I didn't really want to leave his arms, but it was true that I was hungry. After all, I didn't remember eating anything after yesterday's breakfast, before we went to the sorcerer.

As I got up from the bed, I could feel Damien's gaze on me. When I turned to look at him, he was lying on his side, his head resting on his arm, observing my moves with a smirk. His eyes were full of tenderness. His smile made my heart flutter.

I asked him amused, "what?"

"Just admiring your beauty."

His comment made me blush as I went to the closet and chose a pair of jeans and a simple red shirt before going to the bathroom to get dressed.

When I walked out, Damien had put on jeans and a t-shirt that hugged his chest lightly, hinting at his muscles underneath. He was so perfect, my wolf wanted out. But I kept her in check, I kept telling her we couldn't just tell him he was our mate, since he probably didn't even know it as he was a vampire and not a wolf.

A few minutes later, a knock came at the door. A man brought us breakfast. I noticed he wasn't a vampire, which I found curious. I didn't think vampires would associate themselves with humans. I would have expected to see only vampires in here.

As we sat down to eat, I asked Damien.

"Why are the servants humans? I thought you would have vampires serving you."

Damien hesitated, he looked uncomfortable.

"Well, they aren't exactly servants... My father keeps them as slaves, in exchange for a promise not to have their blood drank... He uses fear to keep them at the palace..."

I was horrified at what I've just heard. Those people were slaves. How could they use them like that? I guess some of the things I've heard about vampires were true... I looked up at Damien, he had a dark look.

He looked at me and added, "when I become the vampire lord, I want this to change. I don't like exploiting people. My father thinks lowly of humans, but I don't." I could see the storm raging in his eyes.

Relieved by his answer, seeing he was not like his father, I smiled. "Good, I like that. Then I'll come and see how you treat your servants when you become the next vampire lord." Damien looked at me, his beautiful smile back on his face.

We started eating and I could see Damien wanted to ask me something, but he was holding back.

I took his hand in mine, feeling sparks as our skin touched. "What are you holding back?"

He looked surprised. I was surprised myself at how easily I could read him. "I can see you want to ask something, so what do you want to ask?"

Damien looked at me. "Well, I know it's probably not something you want to talk about but ... did he hurt you? What did he do to you?"

He didn't need to say who he was talking about. I knew what he meant. Thinking back to yesterday brought bad memories and made me feel uneasy. I felt like I was living all those memories again. I was getting overwhelmed by those feelings, lost in my thoughts, on the verge of collapsing.

Damien stroked my cheek gently with the back of his hand. That touch and the way he was looking at me were enough to calm me down. I wondered; did he realize the effect he had on me? I didn't know but I was glad he was there to soothe me.

Still a little bit uneasy, I spoke hesitantly.

"Well, at first Elwin asked me to lay on the table. I was pretty nervous, not knowing what to expect, shaking. He looked at me like I was a piece of meat. I didn't like it at all. I was scared he would drink my blood or something… But he didn't. He started by drawing blood from me with a syringe. I don't know how much he took but I saw many vials on the table by his side."

As I spoke, I could see Damien's face harden. He didn't like what he heard, I could feel it, but I continued, nonetheless. "I don't know exactly if he was searching for something, but he started to cut my dress in several places. Every time he cut open the dress, he would insert a sort of long pointy instrument in my skin. It felt a little like a needle but I'm not sure what the purpose of this was. It hurt a little, but not too much.

At one point I think he injected me with some kind of drug. My head was getting dizzy, I was not scared anymore, I was rather sleepy, so I guess it was something to make me relax. I remember him holding a big machine over me that emitted a weird sound, but I have no idea what it was doing... Then my memories get a little fuzzy. All this time, all that kept me going, was thinking about you. I was hoping you would come and get me out of there. It seemed like these tests were endless..."

I took some time to think, see if I could remember anything else. I felt so alone and scared yesterday. I really didn't like reliving those memories. I stared at Damien. He looked sad and angry at the same time.

Finally, I added, smiling, "Then you finally came to rescue me. The last thing I remember is being in your arms, when I finally knew I would be all right and could let myself rest."

Damien stayed silent for some time, he was lost in his thoughts. When he finally gazed up at me, it looked like a storm was raging in his eyes.

He spoke in a low voice, "I'm sorry."

I looked at him with wondering eyes. "You're sorry for what?"

He looked distraught. "I... I couldn't protect you... I let him do all of this to you... I'm sorry."

Seeing him like that broke my heart. I didn't want him to be so upset. He wasn't responsible for what happened. "It's not your fault. Besides, you rescued me and took good care of me."

I was trying to make him feel better, but I could see it was not working. I could feel his sadness through our mate bond. Even if the mating process was not completed, and the bond was not as strong as it could be, it was still there, letting me feel some of my mate's emotions.

I took his hand and squeezed it. Damien looked at me but didn't say anything. I guess this was something he had to deal with himself. I wished he would open up to me and let me in. I wanted to know what he thought, what he felt. I wanted to be there for him.

I stood up and went to his side, gently hugging him and told him softly, "don't be too hard on yourself." As I was about to get up to go back to sit in my chair, Damien grabbed me and pulled me onto his lap, hugging me tighter.

"I will make up for yesterday, I promise. I won't let them do experiments on you again. I swear." His voice was shaky, but his eyes were full of determination. I knew he would do whatever it took to keep his promise. "I have faith in you."

I stayed there for a moment, sitting on his lap, my head resting on his shoulder. He needed me close to him and I needed him as well. I felt like this embrace was washing away all the bad feelings and the bad memories of yesterday.

I slid my fingers gently in his hair. I liked how his hair fell down on his back. Damien stroked my back softly with his hand. I didn't know for sure if he felt the mate bond. All I knew, is that right now, I felt loved. I wished this moment would never end.

There was a knock on the door, forcing Damien to let go of his embrace to go and answer. I was left standing by myself. When Damien opened the door, I saw this tall, beautiful vampire. She had red hair and blue eyes.

At first glance she was beautiful, but when you looked a little longer, she looked fake. Too much makeup and fake lashes. She reeked of cheap perfume and her boobs looked like they were about to burst from her dress. I didn't know her, but I couldn't stand her. She entered the room without waiting for an invitation and threw herself in Damien's arms, hugging him.

"Hey Dami baby, I missed you so much!" She told him with a smile.

I couldn't believe my eyes. Did he have a girlfriend all that time and didn't tell me? My heart was breaking apart. I mean it did feel like he was flirting with me. What about this morning? What about what happened just now?

I was a fool. Could it be that I was the only one of us feeling the mate bond? Is it possible the bond was not working fully since he's a vampire? Could the moon goddess be toying with me, giving me a mate I can't ever be with?

A surge of sadness and tears wanted to burst out at this thought, but I kept them in. My legs wanted to give out, but I stayed strong, not wanting to show them it affected me. If she was indeed his girlfriend, I wouldn't give her the joy of seeing me sad. The truth is, I felt devastated.

I looked at Damien. He didn't move as she hugged him, his arms in the air in a surprised position. The girl tried to come forward and kiss him, but he pushed her away, looking annoyed more than anything. His reaction reassured me; I wasn't the only one being annoyed by her. He spoke to her and said, "Ellie please."

She gave him a bewildered look. "What's wrong baby? That's not how you greet me usually." She said with tantalizing eyes.

I was starting to feel really pissed at her. I could feel my cheeks going red from anger. My wolf was getting rather angry, seeing this woman's hands on my mate. A menacing growl escaped my chest.

Ellie looked at me like she was finally just noticing me. "Who the hell is she?" she asked Damien, as she released her hug and pointed at me. Damien didn't answer her but told her instead, "Listen Ellie, you need to go. You and I don't exist anymore."

She stared at him, on the brink of tears. "What do you mean?"

He had cold eyes as he glanced at her. He got closer to her, whispering something to her. He spoke so low that I couldn't hear what he was telling her. But after he spoke to her, she retorted incredulously, "What? You can't possibly be serious?" She turned to me and looked at me with daggers in her eyes.

I didn't know what this was all about but if she was looking for a fight, my wolf would gladly give it to her. She was pissing me off anyway, putting her hands all over my mate. She walked to me and grasped my arm with an incredible strength. I was surprised at how strong she was. I mean, I knew vampires were strong, but I've never really had a close encounter like that before.

Her fingers were digging into my skin, so much that she was holding me tight. I felt disgusted when she touched me. My wolf wanted her away from me and I growled threateningly. She snorted as she spoke to me with her rolling eyes.

"Looks like I pissed your little beastie. Do you want to hurt me little beastie?" she asked me with a tone like she was talking to a baby.

That bitch was looking for a fight. My wolf wanted out and my nails were beginning to grow. I could feel my canines coming out. Soon I wouldn't be able to hold my wolf in anymore.

I tried to pull on my arm so Ellie would release it, but I wasn't able, she was holding it too tight. "You'd better release my arm you bitch, or you'll be sorry when I change," I snarled at her.

I was ready to let myself change into my wolf form when Damien intervened.

"Release her arm," he said looking at Ellie with authority. She looked at Damien in surprise. He gave off so much power and authority that she had no choice but to release my arm.

Damien stepped in between us.

129

"This is pointless... Ellie, you need to leave right away. Nobody needs to get hurt."

She stared at me, her eyes full of anger. Then she looked at Damien, disappointed. "As you wish."

She turned and left the room without saying anything else.

************ Damien's POV ************

I can't believe the bad timing for Ellie to stop by. I mean, she usually drops in from time to time, never really announcing herself. It hasn't bothered me before; I didn't have anyone I held dear to me. So, when she came, I usually enjoyed her presence, playing the role of her lover for a day or two, until she left again. Who knows where she goes or what she does? I never really asked her or even thought about it.

But now, it was different. I didn't want anything to do with her anymore. I wanted to be with Kate, and Kate only. I even told Ellie that Kate is my mate. I know she didn't believe me. But I wanted her to understand, there will never be a place for her in my bed anymore.

I think Ellie was trying to provoke Kate into changing to her wolf form. And god, it was working so well! Kate was really about to snap. Was she jealous? That thought made me happy. Did she like me? Could I be so lucky that she cared about me? This thought lightened my heart as I went to close the door after Ellie left.

************ Kate's POV ************

As Ellie left the room, my wolf immediately calmed down a little. My nails shrank back to their normal size, so did my canines. Damien went to close the door behind her.

"Who was she? Is she your girlfriend?"

He looked at me with an amused look as he walked towards me. "Are you jealous?" he asked with a grin.

Hell, yeah, I was! But I didn't want to say it. I turned my head to the side, not really knowing what to answer. I crossed my arms over my chest, pouted my lips.

"It's none of your business anyways."

131

Damien laughed and wrapped me in his arms, his sweet scent surrounding me.

"There is no reason for you to be jealous. She is ... an old acquaintance. I used to date her, but that was in the past."

Being in his arms like that, I couldn't stay mad, even if I wanted to. Just the touch of him made me feel better about this.

"You dated her? Did you see how fake she looks?"

Damien laughed at my comment. But I was serious. How could he date someone like that? Fake nails, cheap perfume. Nothing looked real on her.

"Still, she didn't look like she knew you were not dating anymore."

He seemed to think a little before answering.

"Well... I did not see her for a while, so I didn't get the chance to tell her everything I needed to, before today..."

I thought about what he just said. That meant his relationship with her was recent... I only hated her more because of this. But the important thing was that it's over. My wolf didn't want to share her mate with anyone.

Damien raised my chin so that I looked into his eyes.

"Are you okay? You're not going to change into a wolf anymore?"

I felt embarrassed by his question. "You knew."

He laughed. "Yes, I knew. I could feel your anger, how far I was. I knew you were about to change."

I guess it was obvious. So that means Ellie knew it too. Maybe she was even trying to provoke me to get me to change. Damien was waiting for an answer, his beautiful gray eyes piercing through my soul. I smiled. "No, I'm fine now."

A knock came at the door … again… I was only hoping it was not Ellie. Damien sighed as he went to open the door. I was relieved to see it was not Ellie. There was a slave at the door. He bowed to Damien.

"My prince, your father needs to see you now."

Damien sighed.

"All right, I'll be there in a minute."

He closed the door and came to see me.

"I need to go see my father. I'll be back in a few minutes. You can wait for me here."

I raised my brow and asked, "what makes you think I'll wait quietly for you?"

He smirked at my question. "I trust you."

He changed into a formal long shirt with a vest on top of it and tied his hair into a low bun. He looked classy in it. I liked it a lot.

He turned to me as I was watching him.

"How do I look?"

"Very princely," I answered with a small curtsey, which made him laugh.

But seriously sexy, I thought to myself. Although I would never say that out loud.

I sat on the bed and watched Damien. He sucked in a breath then turned to me. His beautiful gray eyes looked troubled. I got the feeling he didn't get along with his father. Every time he talked about him, it was with a dark look or to disagree with something his father did. I hoped everything would be all right.

"Wish me luck." He said with a wink.

I smiled at him to give him courage. He smiled back at me and left the room. His smile made me melt. It was unfair that he could hold such a beautiful smile that made me lose all my composure like that.

I sat on the bed and pondered. He was right. I wouldn't leave the room. First off, his room was on the fourth floor, and I had no intention to try to climb down the wall. Second, I didn't know my way around this castle. I would surely get lost or meet some crazy people in the hall, like that crazy sorcerer. Reality was, this was the safest place for me right now. And Damien was the only one that could keep me safe here, surrounded by vampires.

As I waited for him to come back, I noticed there was a desk by the window with art supplies. I really loved to draw, so to pass time, I sat at the desk and started drawing on a few empty pieces of paper. My thoughts kept going back to Damien. I decided to draw memories of Damien and I, putting as much detail as I could. I wondered how much time he would be gone as I continued drawing, enjoying the view from the window.

Chapter 7 (Kate)

Mates

I don't know exactly how much time passed, but at one point, Damien barged into the room. He looked scared. He closed the door behind him and locked it. I stood from the desk and went to him.

"Are you all right?"

I could see nervousness and doubt in his eyes. I didn't know what happened with his father, but it wasn't good.

He put his arms on my shoulders. "We need to go … now!"

I didn't understand what was going on, but my wolf was telling me to trust my mate.

I wished he would share what happened. As I was about to ask him, someone tried to open the door but couldn't, since Damien locked it. I heard a bang on the door with someone shouting. "Let us in!"

What the hell was going on? The banging was getting louder, and I feared the door would break open. Damien grabbed me in his arms and opened the window.

"What are you doing?"

He looked at me. "Getting you out of here."

I looked down to the ground, four floors lower. I shouted to him, panicked, "Are you crazy? We're going to die if we fall."

He smirked at me. "Do you trust me?"

My wolf told me to trust him. I nodded and closed my eyes as he jumped out of the window, with me in his arms.

I grabbed him tight, hiding my face in the crook of his neck. I was expecting the ground to hit at any moment now. My heart was hammering in my chest, and I only hoped we could somehow survive the fall. After a while there was still no impact. I opened my eyes and looked up to see Damien smiling.

We were flying through the air! How could I have forgotten that vampires could fly? I looked around me. It was my first time flying. I clung to Damien as I was a little scared of the height. Damien chuckled and tightened his embrace, letting me know he's got me.

After a few seconds, the fear subsided and was replaced with an incredible feeling of freedom and pure joy. This feeling was incredible! The breeze on my skin was great. I felt so free. It was so overwhelming, I lacked words to describe it. The most amazing part of it all was being in my mate's arms. I was feeling protected and happy, enjoying the view.

We flew over forests for quite some time. Then, Damien descended us as we neared a lake. It was the Sleeping Lake, not too far from my house. I've been here a few times. It seemed like a safe place to land, away from prying eyes. He released me when we got to the ground. "Here, you are free to go now."

His words hit me right in the heart. I couldn't move.

It was what I originally wanted, to get out of that cell and get back to my family. But things had changed, I didn't want to go back anymore. Well, not without him anyways. He was my mate; my wolf would weaken without him. I didn't want to be away from him.

He made a move to turn around, not looking at me. Before he had the chance to, I told him, "I don't want to go."

He looked at me with wide eyes.

"Why? I took you away from your home, abducted you. Isn't what you want to do? Be free and get back to your family?"

I knew deep down he was speaking the truth. But at the thought of not seeing him again, my heart was tearing apart. The war coming between vampires and werewolves. We were "enemies." It's not likely I would be able to see him again.

Tears began to drip down my cheeks at that thought. Damien cupped my face gently in his hand, wiping the tears away.

He spoke softly, "Kate... I don't understand... Why are you crying?"

I couldn't hold this in anymore and I shouted to him, "Don't you feel it? I... I can't leave you! You are my mate!"

Damien froze, he looked at me with astonished eyes. I waited a little, but he wasn't answering anything. As seconds passed by, my heart broke a little more.

I spoke sadly, as he wasn't answering anything.

"I knew it... You can't feel it since you're not a wolf... That's what I feared."

Those words seemed to bring him back to life.

"No! No, I feel it too! I... I thought I was the only one feeling it. That's why I didn't say anything. Kate I can't believe this!"

He embraced me with his arms, pulling me against him, holding me tight. This was the greatest emotion in the world! I was so relieved. Tears of joy began to flow as the sadness faded away, after his confession.

The words repeated themselves in my head; he felt it too! I wasn't the only one feeling it. It worked, even if I was a werewolf and he was a vampire.

My heart was beating fast, enveloped in his embrace, basking in his scent, getting butterflies in my stomach.

I whispered, "Oh Damien, I wished you would have told me that earlier."

He kissed relentlessly my cheeks, my nose, my mouth, as if afraid that I would disappear if he were to stop. He ran his hand tenderly on my back giving me goosebumps. I played in his hair with my hand. I raised myself on my tippy toes and kissed his lips tenderly.

He answered, "If only I had known," before kissing me back, his tongue making its way inside my mouth as I parted my lips.

After we broke the kiss, Damien looked at me and for a moment, I could see his soul through his eyes. He looked at me and whispered, "God you taste so good! I can never have enough of you."

I felt the same way, I could never have enough of him, but then I wondered.

"Then why do you want me to leave?"

He looked away to the ground.

"They want to kill you."

I shouted, "What?"

He explained, "Elwin, the sorcerer who did experiments on you. He said to my father that the heirloom is inside of you… My father wants that power for himself. So, they decided to open you up to get to that power. That's why they were trying to get into my room."

I was shocked. They wanted to kill me. What's all that heirloom story? It would be inside of me? I was incredulous.

"I couldn't let them kill you. There is no way I would let anyone hurt you. The best thing I could do was to get you back to your family, so you would be safe."

I could feel his sadness through my heart. The only way for him to protect me was to get me away from him. This was too cruel; I couldn't live away from him. Why did things have to be this complicated?

I knew he was doing this for me.

"Thanks for protecting me."

He smiled.

"I have to, I'm your mate, I would give my life to protect you."

In this moment, I felt like I was the most precious woman in the world. But I didn't want him to give his life for me. I needed him by my side, alive. I asked, "What about you? Will you be all right? You disobeyed your father, the vampire lord... What's going to happen to you?"

I could see Damien hesitating. I felt the answer was not exactly what I would like it to be. He looked me in the eyes and said reassuringly, "Don't worry about me... I will be fine. Whatever my father may say, he would have a riot on his hands if he were to kill the heir to the throne just like that. And my mother wouldn't like it a lot either. What matters right now, is that we find a way to stop this war."

Right, if we ever wanted to be able to be together, this war needed to stop. Although I didn't feel completely convinced that he would be fine. My wolf was uneasy at the thought that something could happen to him. There was not a lot I could do right now. Rage was building up in my heart. I felt so helpless! I wished I could find a solution. But the only thing I could try to do was to find a way to stop the war.

I nodded to Damien. "Any idea how we can do that?"

Damien pondered for a moment. "Remember I told you that a few years ago, an important book was said to be stolen by the werewolves?"

I remembered him talking to me about this, so I nodded. "I think we should find it and bring it back. I'm not even sure if werewolves have it but maybe you could try looking for it?"

Looking for a book shouldn't be that hard to do, right? "Okay, but what should I do once I find the book? How can I bring it back to you?"

His face suddenly changed. He looked at me very seriously. "Whatever you do if you find the book, do not open it. Legend says it puts a curse on anyone that is not a vampire that tries to open it.

A sort of protection to preserve the secrets of the vampires."

He stopped talking, he was waiting for an answer, to make sure I understood his warning, so I nodded to him.

"I will come here every night, to wait for you. If you ever find it, I will be here. If I'm not here, then something is preventing me from coming."

That sounded like a good idea. Plus, it meant I could easily see my mate every night. My wolf was happy at the thought she would see her mate every day.

Wolves tend to get restless when they are away from their mates for too long. Plus, they weaken if separated for too long. Nobody really knew why our wolves reacted like that when they found their mates. Many think it has something to do with the mate bond needing to get well established at the beginning of the relation.

I nodded to Damien. "Okay, I'll get back here every night then."

Damien nodded too but his face was serious. "Please be careful. My father will not back down easily. He wants the heirloom for himself. He will stop at nothing to gain it and I'm not sure I'll be able to prevent him from doing so."

I felt the gravity of his words. I understood the seriousness of his warning. The vampire lord is the most powerful vampire. Even his own sons feared him. There's no telling what might happen if he would catch me. A cold shiver ran down my spine at that thought.

I grabbed Damien's hands in mine, squeezing them as I peered into his eyes.

"I will be careful; I won't let him catch me."

Damien smiled at me.

"Then I will make sure to come every night to see you."

I knew he had to go back, but I wanted to keep him just a little bit longer. I put my hands behind Damien's neck and pulled him gently towards me. He leaned in and kissed my neck, giving me goosebumps.

I whispered in his ear, "I will be waiting for you, my mate. Please don't forget about me. And don't see that Ellie vampire."

Damien laughed at my last sentence. "I would never do that. I will long for you night and day."

He kissed me tenderly, his lips moving softly against mine. I took a deep breath of his scent that was driving me crazy. In his arms, I felt truly loved. I wished for this moment to last forever, but I needed to get back to my family and look for the lost book. It was my only chance to be able to live freely with my mate. I waved as I watched Damien take flight to go back to his castle.

*********** Damien's POV ***********

I could still taste her as I flew, on my way home. I couldn't describe the joy that filled me when she told me I was her mate. I thought I was the only one feeling it. I was so lucky to have her. I already missed the warmth of her body in my arms and her sweet scent.

I will do whatever I must to protect her from my father. I will not let him cut her open, to get whatever heirloom she might have.

I know I'll be in trouble. I tried to reassure Kate, but I fear what my father might do. Not only did I disobey a direct order from him, I also prevented him from obtaining a power that he believed necessary to win the war. And on top of that, I helped the prisoner escape, and set her free.

I only wished that what I said to Kate was true; that my father wouldn't kill me. I hoped today was not the first and last time I kissed her, and that I would have another chance to hold her in my arms again.

*********** Kate's POV ***********

The way back home was easy to follow, I've been to the Sleeping Lake many times. I knew the path like the back of my hand. The forest was silent, and I could only hear the dim sound of my footsteps. A gentle breeze blew on my skin as I walked.

As I approached the house, one of the lookouts saw me and ran to meet me. He took my hands in his and eagerly inquired, "Kate! You're safe! Where have you been? How did you escape?"

He stopped talking and his eyes went wide as he realized. "Oh my god I need to tell your parents!"

I didn't even have time to answer anything, he was already rushing inside the house to see my family. As I was about to open the door to get inside, the door opened itself and my parents were there with my brother, running to greet me. They all embraced me, and I realized how much I've missed them. Their hugs warmed my heart.

I followed them inside and we all sat in the living room to talk about what had happened. I told them about being abducted, about having been questioned, tested. I told them about this one vampire being kind to me and taking care of me and setting me free. I skipped the part about the mate thing... I also skipped the part about the book as I thought I would be better off searching for it by myself discretely.

After I was done talking, my father finally said, "I'm so glad you're back, my daughter. When the war starts, you tell us which vampire saved you and we shall spare him."

I looked at him with wide eyes as I repeated, "War"?

My father looked at me. "Of course! They trespassed on our territory, they attacked us and kidnapped you. You can't possibly think we'd let them get away with all of that."

Right, I thought… From his point of view, vampires broke the pact. But from the vampire's point of view, we broke the pact a few years ago. This was all mixed up. I guess finding the book would be the key to solve this puzzle once and for all and find out what really happened.

I looked around the room and noticed my mother, my father and my brother Will were there. But my sister Bianca was not.

"Where is Bianca, she's not there?"

My brother didn't answer and looked away from me. It was not like him, something was wrong.

Finally, my mother spoke, "Your sister passed out the day you were kidnapped. She has not woken up since that day. She's in her bed with Steven by her side."

My heart fell apart. I couldn't believe this! My little sister, that I loved so much! I had to see her.

Holding up the tears that wanted to come out, I rushed to her room right away.

I opened the door. The room was silent, and her bedside lamp was on. Steven was asleep in a chair, his head and arms stretched out on the bed, next to my sister. As I entered the room, Steven woke up. He looked at me and smiled, "Hey! You're back! Glad to see you're safe," he said, without getting up from the chair.

He looked exhausted, like he had barely slept the last few days. I came closer to the bed and sat by Steven's side.

"How is she? What happened?"

Steven shrugged his shoulders.

"Nobody knows exactly what happened. The night we were attacked, we were all busy fighting off vampires. After the attackers decided to back off, we heard a loud sound coming from her room. We rushed upstairs to find her unconscious on the floor. She's been like that ever since."

So many questions popped into my mind. I thought back at the fact I was put unconscious by Damien and Arius that night. Did a vampire do that to her? I mean, I woke up the next morning so it would have to be something else, right? I was feeling so helpless. I loved my sister so much!

When we were little, we used to always play together. She's three years younger than me. With her blond hair and icy eyes, she used to look like a doll. I remember when we would play tea party together. She was my best friend.

When I look at her now, it seems like the life had been sucked out of her. Yes, she's still breathing, but she rests motionless. How I miss the way her smile lightened the room! Or the way she would come and hug me. I wanted my sister back! There was not a lot I could do right now to help, but I swear I will find a way to get her back.

For now, the least I could do was to watch over her. Maybe Steven could get some rest a little, as he looked so tired. I spoke softly to him, "I'll stay with her, you can go rest a little."

I heard a low growl coming from Steven's chest, his wolf didn't agree. He spoke desperately, "I can't leave her Kate... She's my mate."

I froze at his words. His mate? He was our cousin! How could that be?

"Are you sure about this? Usually, the moon goddess doesn't mate family members together you know."

"Yes, I'm absolutely certain of it. Remember it was my birthday? I turned eighteen. That's when we get of age and can find our mates. When you guys came to see me, I knew it right away. I can't be mistaken, she felt it too."

I knew he couldn't be wrong. I know what it feels like to find your mate, as I just did. You just feel it inside, your wolf is screaming and wants to come out. There's no way to be mistaken about it. But it didn't make sense. The moon goddess never mates family members together.

As if he read my mind, Steven spoke.

"Since Bianca passed out a few days ago now, they did some blood tests on her to see if they could find what was wrong with her. It turns out they did a genetic test too. And they found out that even though she shares the same parents as you and your brother, she holds different genes. Nobody could explain, even your mother's genes don't match."

154

I was astonished. Never in my right mind would I have thought this could be possible. It raised so many questions! Questions I didn't have an answer for right now. But it did clear one problem, though. "So that's why you can be her mate. You don't share the same genes, so it doesn't matter."

Steven had a proud look on his face and the biggest grin. For a moment … that is, until he looked back at her and whispered, "Now if only she could wake up."

I sat down, defeated. I needed to find a way to get my sister back. I also needed to find the vampire's stolen book to stop the war. All of that so I could finally get back to my mate. It felt like I had to climb on top of a mountain or something. This all seemed too much for me to handle. I didn't know if I had it in me to do all of this.

Two people I loved with all of my heart needed me more than ever. I hoped I wouldn't let them down. I hoped I would be strong enough to hold up to their expectations. I mean, I was the Alpha's daughter, so I was strong, right? I could do anything right? I tried to convince myself, but I was doubting myself.

I was lost in my thoughts, watching Steven and my sister. My thoughts wandered back to Damien. How I missed him, how I felt strong and protected with him by my side. I could take on the world with him. He was so sweet, always caring for me.

I remember how he took care of me after that crazy sorcerer did experiments on me. And that's when it hit me! That crazy sorcerer! Right! Surely, he must know things about magic, sicknesses and spells. He probably can help with my sister! Well … that is, if he agrees to help, which seemed unlikely. Unless … unless I have a vampire prince for a mate!

"Do you know if they still have blood they took from her?"

Steven looked at me with questioning eyes. "I think there's a vial or two left … why?"

I was full of hope and had a hard time hiding my enthusiasm.

"I think I might know someone who can help us find out what's wrong with her. But I need you to keep this a secret. Promise?"

He smiled at me. "Anything to get my mate back by my side."

He told me the blood samples were kept downstairs in the small lab at the end of the corridor. The lab where nobody is supposed to go. Yeah right, like I would let that stop me, I thought to myself.

I hugged him and went to my room. Tonight was getting late, I would have all the time I need tomorrow to get the blood sample.

I went back to my room and went straight to bed. I missed Damien. This morning when I woke up in his arms, that's how I want to go to sleep too. I should have thought of asking for his shirt or something that smelled like him so it would help me go to sleep.

My wolf was feeling uneasy, she wanted to get back to her mate, and make sure he was fine. But I couldn't, so I tossed and turned, thinking of Damien. I tried to see if I could connect to him, through my thoughts, as they say that mates can develop the ability to speak to each other through their minds. But I guess our bond was not strong enough yet. I still hoped that he would know I was thinking of him. I finally fell asleep, exhausted.

When I woke up, the sun was already shining. I overslept, but I guess I needed to rest. I stopped by Bianca's room to see if anything had changed. I found Steven at his post, eating breakfast on the side of the bed.

Then I went straight downstairs and found my brother and my parents. Being able to hug them was nice, even though I still missed my mate.

My brother and I promised we would tell each other if we found our mates. I still haven't told him. But when we made that promise to each other, we thought we would have wolf mates... Now that mine was a vampire, I wasn't so sure anymore I should tell him, or how I would tell him. I decided to let that slip away for the moment and to concentrate on the task at hand.

After eating breakfast, everybody was busy. It was the perfect time for me to go to the lab down the corridor. I tried to be careful not to make a sound.

Especially since I lived in a house full of werewolves with a heightened sense of hearing. The good news was that I was also very skilled at being stealthy.

I opened the door to the lab and scanned my eyes across the room before entering; it was empty. I carefully closed the door behind me. A ray of light was filtering through the closed blind. There was a lot of research papers and computers. Finally, on one desk, I found what I was looking for. There were a few vials of blood in a tray and some of them were labeled "Bianca."

I reached for the tray nervously, scared someone would hear me. Did they have security cameras in here? I surely hoped not. Holding my breath, I took two of my sister's vials of blood and put them in my pockets. I carefully exited the room, trying to be as stealthy as possible.

When I got out of the lab, I stumbled on Uncle Zach, who saw me exit the room. Crap! I thought to myself. I got caught. What is he going to say? What should I do? My heart was hammering in my chest.

Zach looked surprised to see me.

"Hey! Kate! What a pleasant surprise! I didn't know you were back home."

Phew! Was I mistaken? Maybe he didn't see me coming out of the room? Maybe he wouldn't say anything? I decided to play it cool and answered, "yes, I came back yesterday! One of the vampires set me free."

My uncle hugged me tight. I always loved Zach; he was the best.

"I'm so happy to know you are safe, sweetheart."

I smiled at him, but then he added, "what were you doing in there? You know it's a restricted area, only authorized wolves can go in the lab."

Dang! He saw me. I had to think of a reason and fast. I told him, "Hum, I was just looking for something."

Yeah ... not the best reason I know, but it's all I could think of on the spot. Thinking under pressure is not my forte.

Uncle Zach asked me, "And what would that be?"

"Huh ... a book! I was looking for a book on vampires."

He looked at me with doubtful eyes as I grinned, playing innocent.

"You know books are kept in the library, right? Although I highly doubt we have any books on vampires. It might still be worth a look."

I facepalmed my forehead to play the game.

"Right! Where did I have my mind?"

Zach laughed at my answer. "Come, let me go with you."

I don't think he really bought my story, but anyways, we started walking towards the library.

I was happy to walk with Zach. Growing up, I always could speak to him when something was wrong. He was a confidant, and I knew I could trust him with almost anything. Maybe he could give me some advice about the fact my mate was a vampire. Although I wasn't really sure how he would react if I were to tell him.

"Hey Zach ... can I ask you something?"

Zach raised a brow. "What is it?"

I wasn't really sure how to address the subject. "Did you ever find your mate?"

Zach stopped walking for a second. He pondered and made a weird face. "It's strange, I can't quite seem to remember, but I don't think so, I could never forget something that important."

Huh, that's too bad I thought to myself. I wanted to ask a few questions.

"Why do you ask?"

I didn't want to tell him my mate was a vampire; I wasn't ready yet.

"What should you do, if you find your mate, and you realize it's someone your family wouldn't like?"

Instead of answering my question, Zach looked at me with a teasing face.

"Did you find your mate Kate?"

His unexpected question got me blushing and I couldn't answer anything. He looked at me and smiled.

"The moon goddess blesses us with one mate only. Whoever she picks for us, we need to accept him, and so does our pack and family. You need to follow your heart. If you love him, then so will we."

Those words warmed my heart and gave me hope. A hope that someday I might be able to live happily with Damien.

While walking, we arrived at the library. I gave a warm hug to Zach, thanking him for his advice. He winked at me and told me before leaving.

"I'll always be there for you sweetheart. I can't wait to meet him."

And with that, he turned away and disappeared.

*********** Damien's POV ***********

What time was it? I lost track of time. I was locked in the dungeon. When I came back yesterday, I got apprehended by the royal guards right away. I was accused of treachery against the vampire lord. I haven't eaten or drank anything; I haven't been able to sleep as they made sure to wake me up every time I fall asleep.

They've been asking me about Kate. They want to know where she is, so they can get her and open her up. There's no way I'm giving them that information. I don't care how much they torture me. I will not talk. I know Father has sent squads of assassins to search for her. I can only hope they won't find her...

I've been hit and whipped. I've blacked out a few times. My skin hurts. I'm so thirsty I could drink anything. My clothes are torn from the torture. The only thing that keeps me going on is thinking about Kate. I don't know when, I don't know how, but I'll get back to her. Even if it's the last thing I do, I'll see her one more time. Wait for me, my little wolf. I'll be there, I promise.

*********** Kate's POV ***********

The library was full of books. I didn't even know we had that many books. I spent most of the day trying to find a book related to vampires, but I didn't have a lot of luck. By the end of the day, I was pretty discouraged.

I decided to take a break, sitting in one of the comfortable armchairs, resting. The red velvet of the chairs felt soft to the touch. I always loved the feeling of velvet. I remember my mother telling me the fairies made them and that's why it was so soft. Even though I am older, and I know it's not how it is made, I still love to believe it.

I watched as the light came into the room through the mosaic window, lighting the room with color and reflecting its drawing on the floor. I could see dust particles shimmer through the light, giving the room a magical vibe.

I heard a familiar voice breaking the silence behind me.

"There's my favorite big sister."

I turned around to see my brother Will. I smiled and went to give him a big hug. His arms felt warm, I was happy to see him.

"So that's where you've been hiding all day! What happened to you? It's not like you used to spend days reading books before."

He was right. Although my mother used to read me bedtime stories cuddled in the armchairs, I didn't spend much time in the library growing up. I was more of an adventurous type. I preferred to spend my time in the forest, following my heart's content.

How I wished I could tell him about my mate and the stolen book. We always promised we would tell each other when we found our mates. My brother and I were so close. He was always there for me. Even though he was younger than me, he would always protect me. I was his confidant, wiping his tears, and he was mine. Even though he was a little younger than me, growing up, people often thought we were twins, because we were so close to each other.

I have no idea how he'll take the fact that my mate is a vampire. I'm not sure I'm ready to try.

"I was looking for a book about vampires. You don't happen to know if we have one?"

My brother shrugged his shoulders.

"I'm always training all the time, I never spend time here. I have no idea what books we have. Why are you looking for one on vampires?"

"Oh, just out of curiosity I guess," I lied.

"Does it have something to do with the fact you were kidnapped by vampires?"

I couldn't find the courage to tell him the truth. Not yet. I wasn't ready. I felt bad about it, but I lied again.

"I guess that now that I've seen them up close, I'm more curious about them."

He nodded. "Right, that could prove useful in the upcoming war."

The war... I didn't want to hear anything about it. But I nodded back to him.

Will took a few steps towards me. He studied me for a few seconds. "You know, I can tell when there's something on your mind. You've been my sister for a long time." He added with a wink.

Yeah, there was no way I could fool him. I couldn't hide everything from him, he knew me too well. I decided to tell him half the truth. "Well.... I might have found my mate."

My brother shouted, "What??"

I giggled at his reaction. "Hush, we're in a library," I teased him. "I found him, but I'm not telling you who it is." I couldn't hide my teasing smile.

Will complained, "Aw! Come on! It's not fair! We always said we would tell each other! Who is it? Is it one of the lookups? Did you meet a wolf from another pack? Tell me!"

It made me smile to see him try to guess which wolf was my mate. He could never guess who it was really.

"One day, I'll tell you I promise, but right now, I'm not ready, okay?"

He laughed a little. "All right sis, but I want to be the first to know!"

I giggled, "Of course you'll be the first."

He was about to turn and leave, but then he looked at me again. "You know I'll love him right away. Just tell me when you are ready." He winked and walked away.

If only he knew who my mate was, he'd understand why I'm hesitating. Everything in its time. For now, it was time we all sat for supper.

As the day passed by, I was getting happier. I knew soon would be the time for me to go meet with Damien. After eating I went straight to my room to freshen up, making sure I was all pretty. I felt like I was going on a date. My heart was beating fast, and my wolf was getting rather impatient.

Chapter 8 (Kate)

Bonded by passion

Soon after, I departed for the Sleeping Lake. The moon was slowly rising in the sky as I waited for Damien to arrive. He hadn't told me an exact hour he would come but I knew he would be there soon. As I watched the sky, looking for him, I remembered his beautiful gray eyes. The way his hair fell back over his shoulders and down his back. The way his beard framed his face so perfectly and his cute mustache. I couldn't wait for him to arrive.

As minutes went by, there was still no sign of him. My wolf was beginning to worry. I tried again to see if I could speak to him through my mind, but I still couldn't.

What if he forgot? No, I was sure he couldn't forget.

Maybe he decided he was better with that fake Ellie vampire girl? No, I couldn't believe it.

He was feeling the mate bond, nothing could replace that. Then maybe something happened to him. That was what worried me the most. The more time went by without him arriving, the more I worried.

It was getting rather late, and I was getting really tired. I was about to go back to the house even though I didn't want to, when finally, I saw him! Damien, he was coming this way. When he landed a few feet away from me, I could see he was hurt. My wolf immediately went into defensive mode as she wanted to protect her mate.

I ran to him and hugged him tight.

"Oh my god! Damien! You're hurt! What happened to you?"

I took a step back to take a better look at him. He looked pale and tired. He had chain marks on his arms. His clothes were torn apart, and he looked like he had been whipped.

Damien fell to his knees as he leaned into my arms. He whispered, "Oh Kate! How I've missed you!"

My heart warmed at his words and a low purr escaped my chest. I could hear his heartbeat against mine. But my wolf still wasn't happy. He didn't answer my question, so I repeated, "Tell me who did this to you so that I can give him what he deserves."

Damien looked at me.

"After hearing that I let you go, my father imprisoned me yesterday as I came back. He whipped me and beat me. He was trying to make me talk and reveal where you were. I've spent all day locked up, chained up, didn't have anything to eat or drink. But then, finally, my brother came and freed me. I knew you'd be waiting for me, so I came straight away."

I couldn't believe what I was hearing. How could a father be so cruel? My wolf was feeling annoyed, she couldn't go against the vampire lord, he was way too powerful for us.

My mate had been in danger, and I couldn't do anything. At the same time, it was my fault he was punished. I felt terrible for everything that had happened to him. Tears began dripping on my cheeks as I told him softly, "Damien, I'm so sorry for what happened to you."

He wiped my tears away with his hands and replied with a voice full of tenderness, "It's not your fault Kate. Don't take this up on yourself. It's like the other day, with the sorcerer, I couldn't protect you."

I laughed as he said that. "What good mates we make."

He burst out laughing at my comment. "I guess we'll get better at it."

His laugh was like music to my ears.

"Yesterday, you were thinking about me, weren't you? I could feel it in my heart you know."

I was happy he was able to feel it.

"Yes, but I tried to reach you with my mind, but I couldn't."

Damien cupped my cheek tenderly. "Patience my little wolf, patience. It will come."

I loved when he called me like that, "my little wolf." I think it sounded so special, so cute.

We sat in the grass, by the lake shore as we talked.

"Did you find out anything about the book?"

I shook my head.

"No, I spent the day looking through books in the library but couldn't find anything related to vampires."

Damien sighed at what I said.

"Don't worry, I'll continue searching for it. In the meantime, I need your help with something."

He looked at me with curiosity as I pulled out of my pocket my sister's vials of blood.

"This is my sister's blood." I explained, "she's been unconscious since the day you came and took me. Nobody's been able to wake her up. I thought maybe you could ask your sorcerer to take a look and see if he has something to make her wake up."

Damien looked thoughtful. He took the vials and put it in his pocket.

"Right, good idea. He owes me for doing tests on you anyway. I'll make sure he collaborates on this."

The night was getting pretty late. We stood up, preparing to say our goodbyes for the night. As he got up, Damien lost his balance and almost fell to the ground, his eyes turning red. I grabbed his arm before he reached the floor.

"Are you all right?"

He looked tired and feeble, and his eyes didn't turn back to their usual gray. He was also breathing more heavily.

"I think... I think I used up too much energy flying all the way here, after being beaten and whipped, without eating and drinking for a day..."

I was truly worried for him; he didn't look well. I could feel it in my body, through our mate bond. My wolf was getting rather uneasy. She wanted to care for her mate.

"What can I do for you?"

He looked at me and I could see he was fighting with himself, his eyes shifting to my neck.

"I need ... to drink blood."

I was shocked. I never saw a vampire drink blood. And more so, my guess was that I was to be involved in this, which meant my blood. At the same time, I couldn't leave him like that. I doubt he could even go back to his castle in this condition. It was my chance to do something to help my mate. I didn't really know what to expect, I was scared.

"... Will this hurt me?"

He shook his head.

"Not really, I'm not going to drink all of it, it's not like you're my prey, you are my mate. These are completely different things."

I didn't really understand what he meant, and I guess it showed in my face because he continued.

"Usually, vampires do not drink blood from another vampire. But when we find our mate ... well, we sometimes drink each other's blood."

I was astounded as I repeated slowly, "You drink blood ... from your mate?"

He laughed at my question and came closer to me, hugging me tenderly, caressing my back with his hand.

He explained, "When we drink blood from our mate, it is considered one of the most intimate sharing we can have. It's a passionate moment and I swear to you, you will like it. With this sharing, you can get so much closer to your partner, for an instant, feeling his love inside of you, truly understanding him... But of course, I don't want to force you, you don't have to... I could also just find an animal so I could feed and get back home."

I stayed in his arms for a moment, thinking back at what he just said. It didn't sound too bad. And my wolf was kind of into this "mate intimate sharing passion" thing. If this meant so much to him, if it was meant to bring us closer, then I really wanted to do it. Having a mate from another kind means you must learn the cultures and traditions, right?

I looked Damien in the eyes. "Okay, let's do this."

He looked at me, surprised. "Are you sure about this?"

I nodded as I raised myself on my tippy toes, wrapping my hands behind his neck and whispering into his ear, "Yes, my mate."

I kissed and licked his earlobe, making him groan softly, before going back down. He purred in a low voice, "You don't know how much I yearn for you." I could feel all his love and passion in his words.

Damien put his hands around my waist and started to kiss me tenderly. His lips were soft. He smelled so nice; this scent of his was driving me crazy. I ran my fingers in his hair as we kissed. He tasted so good I couldn't get enough of him. Damien was running his fingers across my back slowly, sending shivers down my spine. A low purr escaped my chest as he licked my neck giving me goosebumps. He stopped for a moment and smirked.

I looked at him, he had a flirtatious look in the eyes. My wolf wanted to come out and I had a hard time keeping her in check. I involuntarily spoke, "mine." It was possessive, almost a growl, coming from my wolf.

Damien chuckled a little. "Now and forever, I'll always be yours, my little wolf."

"Then, will you allow me to make you mine?"

I didn't know if he knew what this meant, but I needed to do this. My wolf was screaming for me to do it and I struggled to keep her in check. And, for my sanity, I needed to know he was mine.

He smiled. "Gladly, my little wolf."

He carefully laid me on the grass while kissing me. I felt truly loved in his arms. His hands started to roam my body. I arched against him as he brushed his fingers on my breast. I could feel his arousal through his clothes. My body was craving for more as I was getting wet from all the kisses and caresses. He started to nibble at my lips. I pulled out his shirt, revealing his sculpted chest. God, he was so perfect! I was lucky to have him as a mate. His hands glided down my legs then up my thighs, lighting a fire within me. I couldn't suppress a moan as he stroked between my legs, my breathing quickening slightly as my head tilted back in pleasure and envy.

Damien lowered himself and removed my pants and underwear. All I could think of right now was how much I wanted him. We continued kissing under the moonlight, basked by a warm summer night breeze.

He took pleasure in the fact he could make goosebumps appear so easily on my skin. He groaned as I whispered in his ear, "Damien, take me."

He proceeded to remove the remaining of my clothes, while I removed his pants, but as I was about to remove his boxers, he stopped me. "Not yet." He had a teasing smile.

As I was about to protest, he sealed his lips with mine, kissing me as he inserted a finger between my legs, making me moan while we kissed. He had me panting within minutes and I nearly screamed when he started curling his fingers inside of me.

Damien started to kiss my lips, then slowly got down to my neck. I sensed his teeth brush against my skin, but I was too busy grinding against his hand to even care. I felt a sharp pain as his teeth pierced the skin of my neck. The pain subsided as quickly as it appeared and changed into a wave of pleasure. I moaned under him as he drank my blood. I was roaming his body and stroking at his enlarged shaft through his boxers.

With each swallow he took came a new wave of blissful pleasure. I don't know how much he took but I knew I didn't want it to stop. After a moment I felt his teeth retract from my skin and his tongue linger on the mark where he bit me for a moment. I could feel a purr of satisfaction coming from his chest, causing me to purr back in response.

Damien slowly raised his head and looked me in the eyes. His eyes had returned to their haunting gray color that I loved so much. I could see passion in his eyes, a kind of possessive passion. As if nothing could ever come between us at the moment. I could sense his desire through my veins as I wanted the same thing.

He whispered, breathless, "I love you so much."

I whispered back, "I love you too, Damien."

My wolf was screaming for me to make him mine. I couldn't take this teasing anymore and I begged him, "please, take me."

He finally removed his boxers, revealing his enlarged member. I looked at him, full of desire, wanting him to put it inside of me. I started to thrust my hips at him, making myself clear, causing him to groan as he spoke, "oh god Kate."

Finally, he penetrated me, making me gasp and moan under him.

He started to move between my thighs, sending me waves of pleasure with every thrust he gave. My nails were digging hard into his back as I kissed him to stop myself from moaning out too loud. Damien's hands were holding my hips firmly as he pushed deeper inside of me. I started rocking my hips in sync with him, making him tighten his grip on my hips, "Oh yes!" he groaned.

I could feel Damien pick up the pace just a little. He continued thrusting in and out of me, leaving me panting. As waves of pleasure hit me, my wolf started to get the better of me. I let my instincts take control of me. She wanted to mark him, making sure every wolf would know he was ours. Slowly, I began licking my mate's neck, finding the spot where the neck meets the shoulder. That sweet spot, so inviting. All my instincts were guiding me to it. I didn't have to search, I just knew.

Damien growled as I licked him, thrusting even deeper inside of me, making me gasp loudly.

I let my canines grow just enough, so I could bite him on the neck. This was it, there was no turning back. I bit him carefully, just enough so that my teeth pierced his skin. I heard him gasp with pleasure as I bit him, his thrusts getting deeper and slower. I let my teeth into his skin for a moment, while we rocked together, united as one.

As I removed my teeth carefully from his skin, something snapped inside of me, sending me into a bliss of pleasure as I screamed his name. The only thing I could think of right now was clawing and holding tight at the man I loved. Over and over again as I came. A few moments after, his thrusts began to get deeper and sloppier as I felt his body shake and heard him growl loudly before he came.

We stayed there for a moment, listening to each other's heartbeat, resting in each other's arms, basking in love. He looked at me, I could see my reflection in his eyes.

"I am so in love with you, you have no idea," he whispered to me.

I smiled at him as I answered, "I love you so much Damien, I'll always be by your side."

He smiled at my remark and touched his neck.

"I've never been bitten before. Can't say I didn't enjoy it," he added with a smirk.

I watched the mark on his neck. The mark that will stay there, to show everyone he was my mate.

I laughed a little at his words.

"That mark shows that you're my mate, all the wolves will know. You and I are bonded forever as mates now."

Damien thought for an instant before replying, "I'm lucky to be with such a perfect mate forever."

I looked at him and noticed that all his earlier wounds and marks from being imprisoned and beaten had disappeared.

"Did all of your wounds suddenly disappear?"

He blushed a little from my question.

"Well, when we drink fresh blood, our powers are enhanced, including my healing power. So, when I fed from you, it also healed my wounds."

That was amazing! Wolves did have some sort of healing powers too, but definitely not as strong as this. I looked at his neck, but the mark I gave him was still there.

He saw me looking at his neck and explained, "I would never heal this mark. It's an important one, I'll leave it there, a reminder that my mate is there by my side."

I was happy to know my mark would stay on his neck. He was right, this was an important mark. As for us wolves, this was a sign for all the other wolves that this person had a mate. Other wolves could even know who that mate was with it. It was also a seal for the bond, making it stronger. With this mark, his genes would also slightly change, making him compatible with me so that we could eventually procreate, as to assure the survival of the species. But I was in no hurry to have pups.

I knew that usually, when the male marks the female, the female falls into heat soon after. But I didn't know exactly how it worked when the female marks the male. I didn't really think it worked the other way around. So that meant that I wouldn't have to worry about that for now. Either way, I would find out soon if I were mistaken.

As the night wore on, I knew Damien had to get back to his home. Even though I wanted to keep him by my side. My wolf was reassured, now that he was ours. I wished I could stay in his arms forever. We got back into our clothes. Damien held me tight into his arms, and I took a deep breath of his scent. I took a good look at him, trying to engrave all his details into my memories before he left. With any luck, now that the mate bonding was complete, I could keep a link with him when he was gone.

Damien leaned towards me, kissing me on the lips. His lips were soft and luscious. I kissed him deeply, tasting him as I could never get enough of him. Then I watched him fly away, as he went back to his home, my thoughts lingering on what had just happened between us, still feeling the bliss of having found my mate, knowing I would soon see him again.

Chapter 9 (Damien)

Allies

Alone in the night sky, I was flying home, still feeling like I was in heaven from what had happened between Kate and me. Never in my life have I felt so complete. I had drunk blood countless of times in my lifetime. I usually prefer to drink from bottles. I have drank blood from animals and even sometimes humans. But never did it feel like when I drank blood from my mate. I mean, wow! I was speechless. This warm feeling, like I could feel her love from inside of me, completely taking over control of me. It was like if, for an instant, I could actually feel her inside of me, understanding her feelings, her worries, all of her. For a moment, I really understood why they say mates are our better half and how they complete us.

Then my thoughts lingered on what happened after. Sharing this intimate moment with her, showing her my love and passion. I never knew I could feel like that for a woman. There was this need I have inside, a possessiveness that I never knew existed in me. I wanted to keep her to myself. Never in my life did I want to make love to any other women either. She was the one for me. I had no doubt in my mind. When she bit me on the neck, it felt so good. I'm the one who usually bites other creatures, that was a first. I almost came as she bit me, it was so good it's hard to describe.

From the knowledge I had on werewolves, I knew this biting was something very important to them. I felt so proud she chose to live this moment with me. I will cherish this mark forever as for me, it also represents her love for me.

I flew home in no time. The blood I drank gave me such a burst of energy. I've never felt like this before. I went straight to my room.

When I opened the room, everything was upside down. My clothes and the clothes I got for Kate, lying everywhere on the floor. Paper scattered everywhere. There was not a drawer left untouched.

As I stood there, speechless, I heard my brother Arius coming behind me. I turned around to see him close the door behind us.

"Dad had your room searched," he explained.

He got something from behind him. It was a notebook full of drawings, drawings of me and Kate. She must have done them while she was waiting for me the other day. I took the drawings and looked at him, baffled.

"When I heard dad had asked the guards to search your room, I volunteered to help them. Luckily, I found these before them. You would surely be dead if I hadn't found them first."

He was right. My father surely would have killed me if he saw those drawings. Kate drew them with great details, showing us lying together, kissing, loving each other. Never would my father allow this. My brother and I didn't always get along very well, but he was still my little brother. And to think he just saved me. I was so grateful.

"Why did you do it?"

Instead of answering, he pointed the drawings.

"I think you have some explaining to do first."

I sighed. He was right. I owed him an explanation. I started talking, not really knowing where to start.

"I don't really know how to explain this other than … she's my mate, Arius. She's my mate and I love her with all of my heart."

My brother stayed there, thoughtful.

"Huh, I didn't know it could work between werewolves and vampires."

He winked at me, "but I had an idea there was something going on between you two."

I was surprised. I didn't think my brother would take it so easily.

"I thought you would be angry if I told you."

Arius looked at me, surprised. "Finding your mate is a blessing. Who am I to judge if your mate is a werewolf?"

I stayed silent for a moment, reflecting on what he just told me.

"Is this also why you let me out of the dungeon?"

My brother's face darkened at my question.

"No, it was because I didn't want Father to do to you what he already did to me."

I looked at him, baffled. I had absolutely no idea what he meant by that.

My brother looked sad and angry as he spoke.

"Years ago, I found my mate. But she wasn't a vampire. She was a human slave at the castle."

I couldn't believe what I was hearing! I never knew my brother found his mate; he never spoke to me about her.

"One day, we were seen together by someone, and father found out about us. That day, he brought us to a dark room. He chained me and forced me to watch as he tortured her slowly. I couldn't move, all I could do was watch, and even if I closed my eyes, I still heard her cries.

And through our mate bond, I could feel her suffering. As if it wasn't enough, he forced me to watch as he finally killed her. Then, as I was suffering from the severing of the mate bond, he had me imprisoned in the dungeon for a week, whipped every day and barely fed."

I watched my brother, mouth agape. I could see him still suffering. I had no words to console him. Silent tears were dripping down his chin as he was reliving those feelings. I got closer to him and hugged him. He finally let his sadness take over, finding some sort of relief in my arms.

When his cries started to slow down, I asked, "how come I've never heard of this before?"

My brother sniffled a little and wiped his tears with his hands before answering in a trembling voice.

"Father told everyone I had been sent to take a vacation for a few days... Mother doesn't even know. And if I were to tell anyone, he would get to me again and god only knows what he would do to me."

I had a vague memory of my brother on vacation, and I remember he didn't want to talk about it when he got back. I could never have imagined that this was what he must have been through. I was speechless. I knew our father was cruel. But I never imagined he would be like that with his children.

You only have one mate in life, and he killed his own son's mate, knowing very well he could never find another for the rest of his life. Not that you cannot have a girlfriend, my parents are married but they aren't mates. But you can never find another person with whom you can share the same bond as mates.

Not only did my brother save me, but he also saved Kate. I could never repay him enough. This was so much for me to take in, I didn't really know what to tell him.

"Arius … if only I had known. I'm so sorry." It was the only thing I could come up with.

My brother looked at me, he had this kind of brotherly love in the eyes. It's been years since I saw him looking at me like that. He touched the mark on my neck and smiled.

"It's okay, you couldn't have known. Just take care of her and don't let father do the same thing to you. It's enough."

I patted his shoulders.

"I don't know if I can ever repay you. But if I can ever do something for you, just say it."

My brother smiled.

"I guess I should have told you sooner. From now on, we'll watch each other's back."

I nodded as I watched my brother get out of my room. I think that was the moment when I was the closest to my brother in all my life.

I still couldn't believe all my father has done. In the light of what Arius just told me, I wouldn't even be surprised if Father invented that stolen book story just so he had a reason to go to war with the werewolves. I was now more than ever determined to find a way to stop this war.

But this would have to wait for tomorrow. What I went through today was beginning to take its toll on me and I needed to get some sleep. I pushed stuff down from the bed to the floor, I'll clean up in the morning. I went to sleep easily, exhausted from my day.

I dreamt all night of Kate. How I wished I would never wake up just to stay in that dream. But as I woke up, I heard Kate inside my mind. "Are you awake? I miss you. Have a good day."

It was her; I was sure of it. Which meant the mate bond was getting stronger and I couldn't be happier. I pushed memories of me and her kissing into her mind, hoping the bond was strong enough for them to reach her.

Then I told her, "I miss you too, my little wolf. I love you so much."

And surely, she must have got them, as soon after, I heard in my mind, "I love you too Damien."

My heart fluttered at those words. My mate could hear me. I wished I could go and see her right away, but I reminded myself that I had stuff to do first.

I started by taking a nice long shower. I had spent the day before chained in the dungeon, being beaten and whipped. My clothes were torn and stained with blood. I felt like it's been ages since I've felt the relaxing drum of hot water on my skin.

After getting out of the shower, I put on a formal black pant with a fancy shirt. I needed to look the part today. I had plans and I needed to look like a proper prince. I even took the time to tie my hair into a bun. When I looked at myself in the mirror, I was satisfied.

Before doing anything else, I began picking up all the stuff that had been turned upside down when they searched my room. I was angry at my father for doing this. But I mostly felt grateful at my brother for saving me.

I took another look at the drawings. I didn't know Kate was this good at drawing. She perfectly portrayed the love we share in her drawings. There would have been no way for me to deny it if my father had got those drawings. I took the drawings and carefully put them in a locked drawer in my bedside table.

I ate breakfast in my room, but the room felt empty now that Kate wasn't in it with me. After eating, I made my way to Elwin's laboratory. When I entered the room, Elwin was doing some experiment with a dead bird and some strange vials. I walked slowly up to him from behind, but he didn't hear me. I cleared my throat, which startled him and made him drop the vial he had in his hand, shattering on the floor and spilling its contents.

Elwin turned to face me. He looked scared when he saw me. "My p-prince," he stuttered, "what brings you here?"

I was bigger than him, so I was looking down at him, taking a serious look. "You told me you wouldn't hurt the prisoner." I said in a mean tone.

Elwin tried to take a step back, but his back was already against the table. My words had the effect I wanted on him, as his hands were slightly shaking from nervousness. "I-I only did the experiments the lord asked m-me to do on her, my prince. N-nothing more."

I leaned up to him so that my face was only inches away from his. "What you did to her was not pleasant it seems. Did you really think having needles inserted in her skin would not hurt her?"

I didn't even try to hide my anger. My chest was tightening and I needed to take a deep breath or I would do something I would regret. I had to remind myself that I needed Elwin's help to find a cure for Kate's sister.

Elwin gulped. I could hear his rapid breathing and see sweat pearls forming on his forehead.

I pulled back just a little before saying, "I warned you. Whatever pain you bring to her, I will make you pay…"

I waited a few seconds to let my words sink in. "But… I'm feeling generous right now."

I looked as Elwin nodded anxiously.

"Yes, my prince. Whatever you need, my prince."

I had a malicious smile on my face. This was exactly where I wanted him to be. I needed him to be scared of me, to comply with anything I wanted him to do. I didn't even think it would be that easy.

I took the vials of blood out of my pocket and handed them to him. He took the vials and looked at me with wide eyes, waiting for an explanation.

"This blood belongs to someone important. But this person has been unconscious for a few days now. You are to find a cure for that person."

Elwin looked like he was already thinking about what he would do with the vials.

"That shouldn't be a problem, my prince."

He looked less scared now and almost relieved that this would be an easy challenge. Good, Kate will be happy when I have a cure for her sister.

Before leaving his laboratory, I got closer one last time to him, and reminded him.

"This stays between you and me. You'd better not deceive me. Understood?"

Elwin nodded, his stress level going up again.

"Of course, my prince! I wouldn't dare deceive you."

As I left his room, before the door closed behind me, I could hear Elwin let out his breath he was holding. I smiled at myself. This was going just as planned.

I was walking back to my room when I came across a tall, beautiful woman. I had never seen her in the castle. She was walking out of my father's room. She was almost as tall as me, wearing a leather miniskirt and a crop top. She had long braided black hair coming down her back. She stopped for a moment when she saw me and smiled. I didn't realize I was staring and wasn't really interested in talking to her, but I wasn't able to get away either.

She made her way to me, staring me in the eyes. As she got closer, I could feel something was wrong with her, but I couldn't put my finger on what it was.

"Oraya, meet my brother Damien."

I was startled and turned around to see my brother; I didn't even hear him approach.

"Damien, meet Oraya, she is the leader of the succubus group father hired."

I turned back to look at Oraya, and when I did, I was surprised to see that the woman I saw earlier now had sharp teeth, bat-like wings and a long, sharp nails.

She was holding out her hand, waiting for me to take it. I was the heir to the throne, and since Father had hired her, I guess I had to be courteous with her. I took her hand and gave her a kiss on top.

"It's a pleasure to meet you, my lady."

Oraya was smiling at me.

"The pleasure is mine, my prince. Sorry if I used my powers earlier on you, I didn't know we would be working together."

So, I thought to myself, she used her powers on me. That explains why I couldn't move away and why I didn't see her true form. Why the hell did Father decide to team up with succubus anyway? They were treacherous and couldn't be trusted. It wouldn't be the first-time demons would deceive their allies. I needed to be careful with them; it was wiser to keep them believing I trusted them.

"I guess those powers of yours will prove useful on the battlefield," I told her to gain her trust.

She smiled at my remark, making her look both sexy and dangerous. I needed to be wary of her and her group.

"Now if you'll excuse us, my brother and I have some matters to attend."

Oraya nodded and her eyes followed me, as I pulled my brother with me to my room. Just as I was getting out of her sight, I had the impression that Oraya had a wicked smile on her face. But when I turned back to look at her one last time, she had already disappeared.

My brother looked a little surprised but said nothing until we were in my room with the door closed.

"What's this all about?"

"Succubus. Really? Has Father lost his mind?"

"He thought we needed the extra force for the war against the wolves, now that we didn't have their family heirloom."

Anger was building up in my chest at the reminder of this war. My brother looked at me and thought for a moment.

"Yeah, I can see now why you're not as eager as you were before for that war to happen."

I was angry and sad at the same time. I had to find a way to prevent this war. Now with the succubus on our side, I was scared more than ever to lose my precious Kate.

"I will protect Kate with my life, no matter what happens. And besides, you know succubi cannot be trusted."

My brother nodded.

"Yes, I know, but it's not like I can make Father change his mind."

He was also right about that. I was feeling defeated, it was surely showing as my brother added, "don't worry, we won't let anything happen to your mate."

I knew he was only trying to cheer me up. During a battle, anything could happen, and nobody's safety was guaranteed. It did cheer me up a little anyway.

"You know, I want to stop this war." I told my brother.

He nodded as he understood why.

"Let me know if I can help you." He told me before leaving.

Chapter 10 (Kate)

The Hunt

I was sitting in the yard, bathing in the sun, enjoying a lazy afternoon. I had no idea where to look for the book next. I decided to get some much-needed rest.

One thing kept popping in my mind; Lilith. I know I had seen her before, but where? I couldn't be mistaken. Why did her scent feel so familiar?

My thoughts drifted as I watched the clouds, half asleep. Suddenly, I saw Lilith in my mind, she was giving something to Zach. Was I dreaming? The memory was foggy, but I was sure it was not a dream. It must be it! That's when I saw her. But it was so long ago, maybe that's why I didn't remember it at first.

I kept thinking about it, the details were fuzzy. I remember it was night. I know she gave something to Zach, but I don't remember what it was. There's one thing I remembered clearly. Zach and her kissed. They were lovers, I was sure of it! If that's the case, then surely Zach knows something about her. I need to ask him about this.

I got up and decided to go search for Zach. I wanted to hear the whole story from him.

I searched in his study, in the library, I even checked his room, but he was nowhere to be found. I sat in the living room, wondering where to look for him next.

My father came by.

"Hey Kate, how are you my little angel?"

I smiled at him. I loved my father very dearly. He was the Alpha, feared and respected by everyone in the pack. But when we were together at home, he was a tenderly loving father. I was an adult, but I knew that in his eyes, I would always be his daughter.

"Hey dad, I'm doing fine." I stood up and hugged him.

I didn't always agree with him, but I knew that he has to make choices to protect us. He always works for the better of the pack. Being the Alpha must be so hard at times.

I guess it's a burden that I'll have to share someday since I'll become the next Alpha one day.

"Is something on your mind sweetheart?" His question got me out of my thoughts.

"Yes, I was looking for Zach. Have you seen him?"

My father pondered for a few seconds.

"I think he said something about needing to go into the forest. I don't remember why exactly but I guess he's not far."

Good! Now I knew where to find him.

"Thanks dad!" I told him before going outside of the house. I heard him laugh as I exited the house.

I ran outside to the forest. It was sunny and the birds chirped in the trees. I listened carefully, trying to see if I could hear Zach in the forest. It wasn't easy. Even though I had a heightened sense of hearing, Zach was also one of the best fighters of the pack, and so, very good at hiding himself and being silent.

"Zach, are you there?" I shouted as I walked.

I heard a branch crack a little further, so I followed the sound. I began hearing the sound of the water flowing. I was getting at the small river that flowed nearby.

Finally, I saw him! Zach was sitting on a rock near the river, facing the water.

I walked to him. "There you are!"

He turned around. "Hi Kate. Were you looking out for me?"

How could he not know? I've been shouting his name forever, I thought to myself.

"Of course, I was! Didn't you hear me call your name?"

Zach looked embarrassed. He got up. He was at least one head taller than me. "Sorry, I was lost in my thoughts."

"Those thoughts must have been very deep for you not to hear me," I teased him. He laughed at my remark.

"Never mind that. I was looking for you. There's something I want to ask you."

"What is it sweetie?" He asked nicely.

"Do you remember? I was a lot younger. One night, you met with a vampire woman. Her name was Lilith. Her hair is black, she is very beautiful... She gave you something that night."

I watched as Zach pondered, waiting to see if he would recall her. It was taking a long time. I added, "I remember you kissed her."

Zach's eyes widened.

"Surely you must be mistaken Kate. I kissed many women in my life, humans and werewolves. But I never kissed a vampire."

How could he forget? I'm sure it wasn't a dream! I'm sure they kissed. They were lovers! I can't believe this! I was getting frustrated.

"I'm telling you! You were kissing her," I shouted to him.

Zach put his two strong hands on my shoulders and looked me in the eyes.

"Calm down sweetie. I didn't say you were wrong. That name kind of rings a bell in my mind but I can't seem to remember…"

That wasn't good… The only person that could have helped me didn't remember a thing. I crossed my arms on my chest, annoyed by all of this. Zach wasn't doing this on purpose, I couldn't be mad at him. But I was going nowhere fast.

I sighed. "Okay, thanks anyway."

Zach kissed my cheek. "Sorry sweetie, I'll tell you if I ever remember something, okay?"

He looked sincere. I smiled at him and nodded.

I asked him, "are you coming back to the house?"

Zach shook his head. "I still need some time by myself, I'll be back later."

I waved at Zach and started to walk back towards the house.

I was walking for quite some time. I hadn't realized that I was this far from the house earlier when I went to search for Zach. I wondered what he was thinking about. He seemed to have a lot

211

on his mind, being lost in his thoughts to the point where he wouldn't hear me call his name. What could be bothering him like that, I wondered?

I was getting lost in my thoughts myself as I realized suddenly the forest had gone silent. I stopped walking and studied the forest around me. The sun was not set yet, it wasn't normal for the animals and birds to be silent. All I could see was trees everywhere. Yet, I felt uneasy. Something wasn't quite right.

I startled as I heard a crack in the woods. Maybe Zach decided to come back to the house? It was very unlikely. Surely, I would pick up his scent if he was close to me. My heart started pounding faster.

"Who's there?" I shouted, "show yourself!"

As much as I listened, I couldn't hear anything. If someone was there, they were pretty good at hide-and-seek. I couldn't smell anything either. How could that be? Our scent was one of our best senses. The person trying to get me was well prepared, and that scared me even more.

To be attacked by a random stranger was something. But to be attacked by someone who's prepared themselves was way more dangerous. It meant they knew me, they studied me. This was starting to get me really unnerved.

Suddenly, I heard a swishing sound coming my way through the air. My reflexes kicked in just in time for me to evade the blade of a dagger that was thrown at me. Whoever was there wasn't friendly. I didn't see them, but I didn't intend to stay here any longer.

I couldn't go towards my home anymore, as the dagger was thrown from that direction. I started running in the opposite direction.

Right away, I heard footsteps coming my way. I turned my head just enough to see four men running in my direction. They were vampires. They were dressed in black armor. They moved stealthily; I could barely hear them. They were swift, I did not know if I could escape them.

I remember Damien told me the vampire lord would send his guards to get me. Were those the vampire lord's guards? They were not armed like guards. I would say they looked like assassins. I guess the vampire lord only needed whatever "heirloom" I have inside of me. He didn't care if I was taken dead or alive.

I ran as fast as I could. Occasionally, a dagger was thrown in my direction, but I dodged it. I was now way farther from the house as I've ever been. I was outside of the pack's territory. I had no idea if I was trespassing on another pack's territory and was way too busy to worry about that.

I didn't know this part of the forest. The trees were tall and dark. No light from the sun filtered through them. No animals dwelled here. No noise could be heard other than my feet on the ground, my breathlessness and the assassins chasing me. This was no use. The vampires were too fast for me. I couldn't run forever. I decided that I was better off fighting them.

I stopped running and turned to look at them. In a matter of seconds, I was surrounded. Three of them were very tall. The other one was small, almost my size. They looked like they wanted to drink my blood and their eyes seemed to glow in the darkness of the forest. Their nails were sharp, and their fangs were out.

One of them carried a bow and arrows. He looked at me like a hunter watching his prey.

The shorter one had scars and carried a big heavy sword. He wasn't the fastest for sure, but he looked very strong.

None of them said a word. None were needed. The first vampire tried to jump at me, all teeth out, to get at my neck, but I dodged him. I turned around just in time to see the third vampire swing his sword at my head. I fell to the ground, the sword's blade missing me only by an inch.

The fourth vampire grabbed me by the neck and raised me in the air. My feet weren't touching the ground anymore. I kicked in the air and tried to get his hands away from my neck as I gasped for air. Luckily, he was close enough for me to kick him strongly in the stomach. The kick made him lose his grip on my neck and recoil back.

I took a few breaths of air as I fell to the ground. It wasn't long until the second vampire was on top of me. I screamed in pain as he stabbed me in the gut with a dagger. Blood started to gush out of the wound. I wanted to get back up, but the vampire was still on top of me. He lowered himself and licked the blood coming out of the wound, teasing me with a smirk as he did.

That bastard! I was so angry that the pain somewhat subsided. I hit him with my head hard enough that he hissed and backed off.

I started to get up on my feet, the pain in my gut making it difficult to stand. I didn't know exactly which vampire, but one of them sent me flying through the air without even touching me, right into a tree a few feet back. I screamed as my back hit the trunk hard.

I had to face it, there was no way I was winning this fight. I was already bleeding and hurting. And I've seen earlier that I could not outrun them... At least ... not in my human form.

They were all coming my way fast. Quickly, I let my wolf take control of me and let myself change. There was no time for me to think about it. The vampires stopped and looked at me while I transformed. I guess they didn't see werewolves transforming often.

I usually enjoy shifting to my wolf form. But right now, it was painful. The dagger in my gut fell to the ground as I shifted and now blood was dropping from the wound. My back was still aching. I didn't want them to see it, though.

I now stood on my four legs, growling threateningly at them. They seemed to wonder how to deal with me now that I was in my wolf form. I didn't wait for them to figure out and started dashing through the woods. I heard them curse while I ran away.

In my wolf form, I was way faster than in my human form. I knew vampires were fast, but if I had a chance to escape them, that would be it. I ran as fast as I could. I could hear their footsteps behind me. One of the vampires was shooting arrows at me and I had to dodge them while running. One of the arrows hit me in the shoulder blade. I couldn't stop running, despite the pain, or they would catch me. I had no idea where I was going. I just ran as fast as I could, hoping to find a way to escape them.

All I could think of was running. Run. As fast as you can. You need to get away from them. Suddenly, I tripped over a tree root sticking out of the ground. I was too focused on my thoughts and didn't see it. I looked around me and realized that

I wasn't just falling to the ground. There was a cliff, and I was actually falling down the cliff.

As I fell, feeling weightless, one name came through my mind, "Damien."

*********** Damien's POV ***********

What had just happened? I thought I heard my name, but no one was around. I guess I must be tired.

"Was that you, Kate?" I asked through our mate bond. I waited a little bit but she didn't answer. She's probably busy.

I went on with my day, trying to find hints as to where the lost vampire book could be. It seemed there was nothing to be found anywhere. I was getting quite frustrated from that futile search.

Luckily for me, the end of the day was nearing, which meant I could get back to my dearest Kate. I took some time to make sure I looked my best before sneaking out of my room's window to get back to the woman I loved.

As I flew to the lake near her house, I was feeling uneasy. Something was amiss, but I didn't know what exactly. I landed at the lake, but Kate wasn't there yet. I hoped she would come soon, I missed her so much!

The sun was already gone, but still no signs of Kate. I began to worry. I tried to call her through my mind. "Kate, honey, where are you?" I kept trying and trying, but to no avail. Kate wasn't responding. That wasn't good. I was getting rather worried, but I didn't know what to do.

It's not like I could just go to her front door, knock and ask if they knew where Kate was!

The best I could do was try to speak to her through our mate bond or try to search for her. But I had no clue as to where she could be.

I tried to see if I could smell her scent or hear anything, any movement in the bushes. Alas! It was useless. I knew something was not right tonight. I had felt it when I was on my way here, and now I was sure of it.

What could I do? I kept searching but I couldn't find an answer. I was feeling so frustrated! My love was missing, and I couldn't get to her. Rage was building up inside me, but I had no way to release it. Tears were dripping down my cheeks silently. The only thing that made me stay calm, was the fact that she was still alive. Of that, I was sure. Or else, the mate bond would be broken, and I would have suffered its effects.

As I waited in vain, I saw the first rays of light. Surely, there was no way she was coming today. I had to resign myself to get back to the castle. My heart was heavy, I felt nauseous. Taking one last look around, just in case she might be coming after all, I took my leave.

************ Kate's POV ************

I woke up on the shore of the river. The sun was rising. It took me a few seconds to realize that I had shifted back to my human form while I was knocked out. That explained why I was naked. My head hurt like hell. I brought my hand to my head and felt something warm. When I looked back at my fingers, they had a little bit of blood on them. I guess I must have hit my head.

I looked up and saw a cliff. Surely that is the cliff I had fallen off yesterday. My wounds hadn't completely healed, despite my werewolf healing powers. I was sure that I would be dead if I had been only a human. I thanked the moon goddess to be alive.

I got up to my feet. I winced at the sharp pain in my gut, reminding me that I'd been stabbed yesterday. I studied my reflection in the murky waters of the river. My body was covered in bruises, mud and blood. I had scratch marks everywhere. Blood had dried on my forehead.

I had a sharp pain every time I moved my left arm. I remember vaguely receiving an arrow in my shoulder blade while running away from the assassin's yesterday. I reached for my back with my right hand and sure enough, I could feel the end of an arrow pointing out.

I know it's going to hurt like hell but I can't leave it there. I grabbed the arrow with my hand. My heart rate was elevated. I was scared. Gosh I wish I didn't have to do this! Okay, focus Kate, the sooner you pull it out, the sooner it's over. I took a deep breath and pulled as hard as I could. I screamed from the pain. I could feel the head of the arrow move through my flesh. The pain was excruciating and I couldn't hold in tears. I finally heard a gushing sound and felt warm liquid on my back. I was bleeding, but at least the arrow was out. I took a few deep breaths, still shaking from the pain.

Just then, I realized it was morning, which meant that Damien must have waited for me all night long and I hadn't come. How I missed him right now! I tried to speak to him through my mind, but my head hurt too much. I guess I'll need to heal first.

I was dirty, wounded and hungry. I was lost and had no idea where I was. I had no way to climb back up the cliff where I had fallen down yesterday. My head still a little dizzy. I looked around. The river was surrounded by cliffs on each side. On top of the cliffs were tall dark trees absorbing the light of the sun. I couldn't stay here either, no one would find me.

At least that meant no assassins would come here. Why didn't they finish me yesterday? I guess I looked dead enough after my fall. Although they were supposed to get my "heirloom" (whatever that is...) Maybe they lost track of me? Oh well, it doesn't matter. I'm alive and I'd better keep going if I want it to stay that way.

I need to find something to eat but I'm in no shape to hunt. Hell, I don't even know if I'm able to shift to my wolf form right now! My wolf is wounded. She's busy healing herself and me at the same time. I need to keep low.

A cave on the side of the cliff seems like a good option. I ventured into it. It is dark but it does not pose a problem since my eyes can see well into the darkness. From afar, I can hear drops of water dripping slightly. The cold humid air makes me shiver. Although it is summer, there's a drastic difference of temperature between inside and outside of the cave. Being naked doesn't help me stay warm.

At the end of the cave seems to be a passage big enough for me to venture into it. The whistling of the wind seems to come from somewhere deep inside. There might be an exit further! With my hopes up, I started walking, limping on my left foot, taking care to listen to any signs of danger. Luckily, the cave seems abandoned; I wouldn't be in a shape to fight anyone right now.

I have no idea how much time passed, but it seemed like an eternity. After crossing several boulders, I finally see a faint light in the distance.

A feeling of happiness fills me, soon to be replaced with fear. Where does this exit lead me? I sucked in a breath to avoid crying from the pain as I crouch to the ground. I crawled slowly towards the exit, trying to be as silent as I can.

I could hear voices from afar. I advanced to the exit of the cave. After being stuck for so long in the dark, I had to take a pause to let my eyes adjust to the light.

I looked at my surroundings. The cave's exit was in a sunny forest, on the edge of a castle. I knew this castle very well. It was Damien's castle! Which meant I could go see him, he would be able to help me for sure.

I tried once again to talk to him through our mates' bond, but I failed. It seemed the injury to my head was not yet healed. I needed to find a way to get inside.

I stepped outside of the cave. I could see the front gates of the castle further. They were heavily guarded. Merchants were coming in and out of the castle. The guards searched every cart that entered the castle so there was no way for me to hide inside one to gain entrance.

I couldn't climb the walls. Even if my wounds were completely healed, it was too high. There was no back door either.

My only way inside the castle was by the front gate.

I hid myself in the bushes and observed carefully the guards. It seemed that every hour or so, there would be a change in the guards. I guess that would be my best bet. If I was lucky enough, there would be enough commotion to allow me to enter the castle without being noticed.

A noise behind me got me out of my thoughts. I gasped in surprise. I turned around to see a vampire jumping at me. He put his hand on my mouth and pulled me to the back of the castle.

I tried to get myself free, but I was too weak and tired. As we got to the back of the castle, I recognized him.

"Kate! What are you doing here?" asked Arius, surprised to see me.

He let go of my mouth so I could speak to him. I took a step back from him now that I was free.

"Do not come closer," I said, warily. Arius snorted at my answer.

"If I wanted you to be dead, you would be already."

I guess he was right. Still, I had to get away from him. I turned around but he shouted, "Don't go! Please, Damien told me."

I froze at that name. What exactly did he tell him?

He continued, "I will not hurt my brother's mate."

I turned around to face him.

"Then why did you take me back here?"

"You were about to do something stupid."

I looked at him with doubtful eyes.

"You're hurt Kate. You reek of blood. Any vampire would have smelled you. Don't you know vampires crave the scent of blood? There's no way you can pass the guards unnoticed."

I stopped for a moment. He was right. I didn't think about that. He probably saved me.

"I guess you saved me then … thanks."

Arius smiled.

"I know where you want to go. Come, I'll get you to him. He's been worried sick about you." He gestured to me to approach him. I guess it was my best option. I decided to trust him.

Only when he took his coat off and covered me with it did I remember that I was still naked from shifting back from my wolf form. Suddenly I felt so embarrassed. How long had he seen me that way? I guess it couldn't be helped but I felt myself flush because of the predicament I was in.

Arius didn't seem to care, though. He grabbed me in his arms. I could feel that he was as strong as his brother.

"Be silent, my father is still searching frantically for you. We'll get in by the air," he said, as he looked up.

I grabbed his shoulders as he took flight. I'm still not used to this flying. I liked it better when it was with Damien, but I felt grateful to get Arius's help.

In a matter of seconds, we arrived on the fourth floor of the castle.

Arius checked that the way was clear before entering. He kept me in his arms as he walked swiftly to a door. Without even putting me down, he knocked at the door.

I didn't remember the castle very well from my last visit and only hoped Arius didn't deceive me. I remembered that Damien's room was on the fourth floor. But what if he brought me to the sorcerer instead? I waited anxiously for someone to answer the door.

All my fear vanished when I saw Damien opening the door. He looked exhausted. His eyes were red from crying. He was in such bad shape! I had never seen him like that.

His face lightened up when he saw me.

"Kate!" he shouted.

Arius put me on the floor, and I collapsed. My legs refusing to hold me up. I didn't realize that I was this tired.

Damien picked me up in his arms. Finally, I thought to myself! How have I yearned to get back to him.

"Take care of her," said Arius to his brother.

"How can I ever repay you?" asked Damien.

Arius shrugged his shoulders.

"Don't worry about it."

Damien hugged me tight. Before he brought me inside his room, I turned to Arius.

"Thank you so much, Arius."

He smiled at me.

"Get better soon," he said as he left.

Chapter 11 (Damien)

Healing

I couldn't believe the state Kate was in. She couldn't even stand up properly. What happened to her? How did my brother find her?

I had so many questions in my mind. But at least, she was with me. I was so worried when she didn't show up yesterday! I knew something was wrong. That, and the fact I couldn't connect through our mate bond. I cried so much and didn't have any sleep. But a second wind of energy took hold of me.

All of those questions could wait. I had to take care of her now. That was the most important thing to do right now.

I held her in my hands like she could break apart if I squeezed her too tight. I loved her so much! I missed her sweet scent, although right now she smelled like blood. I removed my brother's coat from her and slipped her into a light night gown.

I lay her carefully on my bed. She had scratches all over her body and a big bump on her head which still bled lightly. It looked like she also had a wound to her gut, as I could see a big spot of dried blood. And it seemed her shoulder blade was still bleeding quite a lot. I guess the most important thing right now was to get her healed.

I thought werewolves had healing powers like us. How is it that she's in such a bad shape? I thought to myself. I'm lucky to have her alive if I judge from what I see.

My chest tightened at the thought that I could have lost her. I don't know what I would do if I would.

Swiftly, I went to my cupboard. I was looking frantically for something. After searching for a while, I finally found it.

It was a healing potion Elwin once gave me. As the heir to the throne, you never know when someone might try to kill you to gain access to the throne. Although I'm sure my brother would never do that, I always keep a stock of healing potions just in case. You never know what lurks in the corridors of the castle.

I took the potion and went back to the bed. Kate was still there, looking like she was almost asleep.

I stroked her cheek gently with my hand. She turned her head at me and smiled.

"Here, my little wolf. Please, drink this."

She looked at the potion I was holding and looked back at my eyes.

"What is it?"

"It's something to help you get better."

She nodded and tried to get herself in a sitting position. I could see her wince from the pain. I helped her sit in the bed, trying to lessen the efforts required to do so.

When she was finally sitting, I gave her the potion. She drank it all without questions. I wondered how it tasted, since I never actually had the occasion to try it yet.

Kate smiled at me after drinking it.

"How do you feel?"

She seemed to think a little before answering.

"I'm hurting everywhere... But I'm so happy to be here with you."

I took her hands in mine and squeezed them.

"I was so worried about you! I thought I had lost you."

All the emotions from the past day started to flow back and I couldn't hold up the tears that wanted to come out. It's as if I could finally let out all that I've been holding inside.

Kate gently wiped my tears away. I didn't want her to worry about me. She was the one needing care right now.

"What happened to you? How did you wind up like that?"

She whispered, "assassins."

I clenched my teeth at her words. I knew my father wanted her "heirloom." I didn't think he'd go that far as to hire assassins. I was boiling inside at that thought.

How I wish that I could go and give him a piece of my mind! I was feeling helpless. I knew my father was way too powerful for me to tackle. All that I could do was to nurse my mate back to health and care for her.

I wanted to hear the whole story. I looked at Kate. She looked exhausted. I helped her back into a sleeping position.

"Rest yourself, my love. I will watch over you."

Kate squeezed my hand.

"I love you, Damien."

I watched her as she fell asleep. I hadn't slept last night and was pretty tired also. I knew the healing potion would begin to take effect soon. I laid by her side and let myself slumber, knowing that she was safe by my side.

I woke up an hour or two later. Kate was awake, gently caressing my back with her hand. The touch of her hand made my heart beat strong. I was so lucky to have her.

"You look like you're feeling better."

She smiled at my remark.

"Yes, thanks to your good care."

I cupped her chin and kissed her sweet lips.

I looked at her. It seemed like the bleeding had stopped. The bump on her forehead already disappeared. Only dirt and dried blood remained of her earlier wounds. This healing potion really helped. I grinned at myself.

"We should get you cleaned up."

Kate sat on the edge of the bed.

"I should get into the shower, then."

I shook my head.

"I have a way better idea than that."

She had no idea what I meant. I couldn't hide my smile. I loved playing with her.

She watched me grab her an outfit from my closet with a dumbfound look on her face.

I chose a long blue dress with a flowery pattern. The dress was sleeveless and tied behind the neck. Truly, she will look like an angel in this dress.

I grabbed her hand and gently guided her through the corridors of the castle, after making sure I wouldn't come face to face with my dad or his guards.

I loved how the glossy black and white marbled floor tiles contrasted with the high cathedral-style ceiling. Skylights allowed for the sunlight to enter. The ceiling was decorated with carpentry and artwork. It was a beautiful sight.

At the end of the corridor was the chamber that I was looking for.

I turned to Kate.

"Close your eyes."

She giggled and obeyed. I loved how she had complete faith in me.

"Good girl," I teased her as I opened the door and led her inside.

I closed the door behind her.

"You can open your eyes now."

Kate opened her eyes. I loved the look on her face as she looked around her.

We were in the royal bath chamber. It was a vast room with a big rectangular bath carved into the marble floor. In truth, this looked more like a pool as it was so big. Around the room were various flowers, oils and perfume available to poor into the water.

There were four lion-shaped faucets, one on each side of the bath. At the center stood a round marble slab with all kinds of soaps and shampoos.

Seeing the amazed look on Kate's face was worth taking her here.

I pressed a button and all the faucets started pouring hot water into the bath. I poured a few drops of scented oils and rose petals.

"What do you think?"

Kate sucked in a breath.

"Damien, this place is magnificent."

I smiled at her remark.

"The best part is that we get to bathe together. No one will come here."

We removed our clothes and proceeded into the water when the bath was full.

Kate sighed slightly as she entered the water. Her body glided graciously. I admired her beauty. Her breasts were floating voluptuously at the surface of the water. How I wished I could grace her body with pleasure right now.

Instead, I circled her waist from behind. She rested her back on my chest, relaxing into my embrace.

I started to wash her body, gently scrubbing it with a sea sponge. I watched as her skin returned to her usual beauty, the mud and dirt falling away. I loved the softness of her skin on my fingertips. She washed her hair with the scented soap, leaving a fresh smell of flowers in it.

When we finished washing ourselves, we stayed in each other's embrace. I lavished her body of kisses. There was no sound, other than an occasional moan escaping her lips. She roamed my body with her hands. I seized her breasts in my hands and played with them, taking good care of each of them. I was hard by now, and every sigh of pleasure she made only made it harder.

I couldn't hold a groan when she started to grind against me. She had the devilish smile on her face that gets me hot every time.

We sat on the bath stairs, our bodies still in the hot water. Kate straddled herself onto my thighs. She started to rock up and down, never quite going all the way, leaving my cock only just touching her cunt. Her hard nipples were gliding on my chest.

"Fuck Kate! You're driving me crazy," I groaned.

She kissed me, her tongue dancing with mine.

I moaned as she finally went all the way down, feeling her hotness around me. She was so tight; I had a hard time restraining myself.

We were surrounded by waves in the bath as we made love. Kate increased the rhythm as pleasure hit her. I loved to hear her whine and I couldn't help moving my hips to take her harder.

With each new stroke, I felt her tighten on me, as I went further into her. We continued our endeavors until she screamed my name, her body trembling. I called her name as I climaxed with her.

I held her in my arms as she rested her head on my chest. A soft purr came out of her chest, vibrating through my chest. I kissed her neck, giving her shivers. This was all I ever needed in my life.

In my arms rested the woman I treasured the most. Yet, I couldn't help thinking that I almost lost her.

"What would I do if I were to lose you?"

She raised her head from my chest, looking me with her appealing hazel eyes.

"You will not lose me."

I knew she wouldn't get away intentionally. Yet, nothing guaranteed me she wouldn't be chased by assassins again. I couldn't be there with her at all times.

"Yet, yesterday, I almost lost you. I couldn't even connect to you through our mate bonds."

I could see in her eyes she understood what I meant.

"I guess the mate bond was broken because I hit my head yesterday." I heard in my mind.

I smiled and kissed her. I was so happy to see the mate bond was back.

"It seems you are healed." I pushed through her mind.

"Maybe we should get out of here before the water turns cold. We should go eat in my room." I proposed out loud.

I didn't need to ask a second time. We've been in the bath for quite some time now.

We got dressed and sure enough, Kate truly looked like a Greek goddess in that dress. Her hair rested on her naked shoulders. The dress flowed down to her feet. It was the perfect sight.

We got back to my room. I was feeling grateful that everyone seemed busy, and we didn't meet anyone in the corridors. The only slaves we met would never dare to say anything or question the heir's decisions.

As we sat down and started to eat, I knew that I could finally hear the whole story of what had happened to her.

My heart sank as she told me about the assassins. I was so scared when she told me she'd been stabbed in the gut. The great fall she had probably explains the injury to the head she had and how we couldn't communicate. Did her wolf get hurt as well? I've heard speculations that werewolves had a second soul, their wolf, and that it had a life of its own. I've never really thought about that before... I'd have to ask Kate more about this one day.

I listened as she continued her tale about the cave she's been in, and finally, how she was found by my brother. I made a mental note to try to find a way to repay him. He saved her life another time. I would be forever grateful to him.

After she was done, I pondered a little. If assassins found her at her pack, it would mean trouble. It would mean they've found her and would be back again.

"Were the assassins up to your pack's land? Did they find a way to come all the way there?"

Kate shook her head.

"No, I ventured further in the forest as I was looking for Zach."

I had no idea who that was.

"Zach?"

She nodded.

"Yes, he's my uncle. I finally remembered!"

She looked truly excited, but I didn't understand what she meant.

"Remembered what?"

"I remembered where I saw Lilith."

That explains her excitement, I thought to myself. I was eager to hear about that, since Lilith clearly told her she had just met her.

"When I was little, I don't know how old I was. One day, I came to the lake at night; I used to sneak out of my room and wander at night. I surprised my Uncle Zach, talking with Lilith. I remember it clearly, they were kissing, Damien. They were lovers!"

I couldn't believe what she was saying! My aunt, our best general preparing for the war, would have been a lover with a werewolf? How could it be possible? Then again, a few years ago, she was not the same as today, so could all of this be related?

Kate's giggle got me out of my thoughts.

"You see, Zach was out in the woods when I was searching for him. He was way further than I would have thought. That's how I got to meet the assassins... But you know, thinking back to that day. What's even more interesting, is I remember that Lilith brought something to Zach... But I never got to see what it was."

This was getting more and more interesting.

"Could it be the missing book maybe?"

She shrugged her shoulders. "Maybe, I was really young, so I don't quite remember."

I kept forgetting how werewolves had such little lifespans compared to us vampires. A few years ago, for her, meant she was a little child, as for me, I didn't look a lot different than now. Although we did look about the same age, I was way older than her. Which meant that she would age way faster than me and I would lose her quite rapidly if I didn't find a way to get her to live as long as me... A problem I would have to deal with sooner than later.

"Do you have an idea how old you were when it happened? The book disappeared about eighteen years ago. It could help us see if the timeline fit."

Kate seemed to ponder a bit before answering.

"I guess the timeline fits. I guess it would make sense that I was about five years old. Which could also explain why I had a hard time remembering Lilith, since I was so young."

I squeezed her in my arms while holding her hand to my mouth, kissing it softly on top.

"You are still so young, my little wolf."

She looked surprised. "Well, I must be about your age, right?"

I sighed. "Vampires age very, very slowly, and live for hundreds of years, my love. Actually, I am two hundred and twenty-seven years old."

Kate looked at me, her mouth agape.

"I really hope this doesn't change how you feel about me. As I truly love you with all of my heart."

She looked into my eyes, and I could feel all the love she held for me as she stared at me.

"Damien, I wouldn't have guessed. But this doesn't change a thing. You are my mate and will always be. I only wish I could stay by your side longer, since I don't live as long as a vampire."

I kissed her soft lips, tasting her sweet taste as I let my tongue into her mouth. I spoke to her softly, our foreheads touching.

"All things in time my little wolf. We'll solve this war problem first. We can't have assassins chasing you all the time either. We'll work on your lifespan if possible after, when we are free to be together at last."

Kate smiled and nodded.

"I tried to go talk to Zach, about Lilith. That's why I was seeking him in the woods. He seemed like he had a lot on his mind. But he didn't seem to remember anything about Lilith," she said, thoughtfully.

"It seemed weird that he wouldn't remember. Especially since I remember clearly, they were lovers."

She was right, it was a little weird. Unless maybe he didn't want to talk about it.

"I will go and see Lilith tomorrow, maybe she'll remember him."

Kate nodded. If all of this was true, and I trusted Kate was telling the truth, then something was amiss.

My heart skipped when I heard a knock on the door. I was scared that someone spotted Kate and told my father she was here.

"Get inside the bathroom and close the door," I told her through our mate bond.

She nodded, got up and went to hide in the bathroom. If it was indeed my father, I needed her to be hidden.

I walked nervously to the door. I couldn't wait too much before opening the door or it would be suspicious. I hoped that whoever is at the door wouldn't notice the two sets of plates at the table.

I opened the door, holding my breath.

To my relief, it was Arius.

"Hey! I came to get news about Kate."

"Hush!"

I looked around in the corridor. Hopefully, no one was there.

I pulled my brother inside my room and closed the door.

"You can come out Kate," I told her.

Kate came out of the bathroom, relieved to see my brother.

"Hey Arius." She smiled at him.

My brother went to give her a hug.

"I'm relieved to see you're doing better."

"It was all thanks to you, for bringing me to my mate. And all the good care he gave me."

She smiled as she said that last part. I could feel tenderness in the way she said it. I smiled back at her.

"Don't forget Elwin's healing potion. You would still have a long way to heal if it weren't for that."

Arius laughed.

"Did that thing actually worked?" he asked.

I nodded.

"Just look at her, you'll see how healed she is."

Arius and I always used to joke about Elwin's powers. Not that we thought he wasn't a good sorcerer or anything. He used to give us all kinds of potions. We never really trusted what was inside of it. We never actually saw him do any magic. We always wondered if he was all talk and no action.

But today, after seeing what his potion did to Kate. I was amazed at how well and fast she recovered. I know now that I was wrong. Elwin was a better sorcerer than I thought. I found a new kind of respect for the man.

My brother's words got me out of my thoughts.

"You know you can't stay here."

I didn't want Kate to leave, but I knew he was right. Kate had a sad look on her face. I took her hands in mine and squeezed them.

"He's right you know. If you stay here, people are going to notice eventually. It's only a matter of time before my father hears about you."

She understood what we meant and nodded.

"Plus, I guess your family is going to worry about you being away for so long, right?" I asked her.

Her face lit up as she realized it.

"You're right! They must be searching everywhere for me!"

I looked outside. The sun was beginning to come down already. It would be a good time for me to get her to the lake without being seen.

"We should get going," I told Kate.

She went to my brother and gave him a hug.

"Thank you again for saving me."

He hugged her back and grinned at her.

"It was nothing, you are my sister after all."

I couldn't be happier that my brother got along with Kate like that. I hugged my brother too. After our farewells were told, it was time for me to go with Kate.

Chapter 12 (Kate)

Inner strength

I was in Damien's arms, flying over the forest. I was beginning to get accustomed to travel this way. It was convenient and fast. I let my thoughts drift away as we flew, basking in Damien's sweet scent of honey and musk.

I still couldn't believe how lucky I was that I found Arius outside of the castle this morning. It would have been anyone other than him or Damien and I would have been dead. In the state I was, I had no chance of running away or fighting back.

I wasn't sure at first if I could trust Arius. But when he said that Damien told him about us being mates, I knew that it was safe.

I'm just so happy to know that Damien's brother approves of us, and that he's an ally. It's a relief! I hope everything goes well when I tell my family about Damien. I still don't know how I'm going to do that. I know that I'm going to have to do it at one point, but I'm not ready yet.

I don't remember a lot from before Damien gave me that healing potion. I remember the strange taste of strawberry and mint it had. I just know that when I woke up after, I could feel that my wolf was feeling better. She was back up, happy to be with her mate, wagging her tail.

I squeezed Damien's arms as we flew. He squeezed back. I loved him so much! Once again, he was there when I needed it. He took care of me. And probably saved my life! I hoped that one day, if he needs it, I'll be able to return the favor.

As we neared the lake, I saw people walking through the forest. Damien cursed.

"I think they're looking for you. We can't land here."

I've been gone for almost two whole days now. The entire pack must be looking for me. It's going to be hard to find a place to land without being seen.

As if he could read my thoughts, Damien spoke.

"I think I know just the place we can go."

He made a sharp turn to the right, to a part of the forest where I never really ventured. It was farther than our pack's territory and we didn't usually need to go that far.

Damien landed us on the edge of a big cave. It was very tall, and I couldn't see anything past the first few feet as there was no light inside. Small crystals could be seen growing through the rocks. It truly looked magnificent! Outside, the cave was partly hidden by a waterfall. This was a perfect landing spot for us. It was not far from my pack's land, so it would be easy for me to get back home.

I hugged Damien.

"Thank you, my love. This place is breathtaking!"

"It is said that this cave is the lair of Ladon, a dragon with a hundred heads."

I gasped as I remembered the legend. It is said that Ladon was the son of the goddess Echidna and the titan Typhon. It was a fierce dragon. If this was indeed his lair, I should be careful not to wake him up. I didn't really believe all those legends … but one might never be too cautious.

"I'd better not wake him up then."

Damien laughed at my remark.

"Come, then."

He took me gently by the hand. I loved the way our fingers joined together. We walked to the edge of the woods a little further, at the border of my pack's territory.

I didn't even have the time to set foot into the territory before two strong arms grabbed me from behind and pulled me away from Damien.

"Kate!" Damien shouted as he ran, trying to catch me.

I recognized the scent of the person holding me. Could it really be him? What was he doing so far away in the territory?

"Will! Let go of me!" I shouted to him.

He threw me to the ground without a word. A second later, he was into his wolf form, growling fiercely at Damien.

I wanted to do something, but I didn't know what I could do. This was wrong! I didn't want my brother and my mate to fight! Couldn't he smell it? I marked Damien as my mate. How come my brother didn't see it? He should be able to. Is he in a bloodlust or something?

Bloodlust is bad. When a werewolf gets enraged, he enters a state called bloodlust. When you are in bloodlust, you can't see straight. You have problems getting your thoughts right. Your wolf takes full control of yourself. Most of the time, this continues until the source of the rage is killed, or until you get yourself killed or wounded enough that you cannot fight anymore. It was a very serious condition. Every wolf knew not to let go that far.

I couldn't understand how Will could be in such as state. Could it be that he was *that* worried about me?

I watched helplessly as Damien put himself into a defensive state.

I felt it through our bond. He didn't want to hurt him. He only wanted to defend himself. He was being nice, because of me. I only hoped he wouldn't get himself killed by doing so.

Will took a lunge at Damien, trying to bite him. Damien avoided his attack. Will continued to attack relentlessly, but Damien kept dodging him again and again.

I couldn't watch this, but I couldn't do anything. If I tried to join the fight, I would surely get hurt.

I screamed, "Will, no!" but my brother didn't seem to listen to me. He just kept attacking Damien all that he could.

I guess the only thing that could reach him in this state would be… "Will, stop! He is my mate! Stop please!"

That's not how I wanted him to learn about Damien, but it seemed to work. Will stopped attacking. He looked surprised, even in his wolf form. He was staring intensely at me.

He started to slowly approach Damien, but he stepped back.

"Damien, it's going to be okay. Let him come to you."

Damien looked at me, then he looked warily at my brother. I could understand his apprehension. He had just been attacked relentlessly and now I was asking him to let this wolf approach him.

He finally decided to trust me and do as I ask.

Will was not showing any signs of hostility anymore. The bloodlust was over, I guess the surprise of learning Damien is my mate was enough to shake him out of it.

He came just a few feet away from Damien. He was taking in his scent, observing him. I knew he was gauging him. Trying to figure out if what I said was true.

Finally, he looked at his neck and saw the mark I left on Damien's neck. I think that's when he realized.

He ran behind a bush nearby and changed back to his human form.

"Here we were, all worried about you! And you were fooling around with a vampire? All that while your sister is still unconscious? Pfff! I thought my sister was better than this."

He looked disgusted as he shouted at me.

"Will, please! It's not like you think!" I pleaded.

"Save it for someone who cares!"

He made a move to get away, but I shouted.

"Will, please, I'm not ready for everyone to know about my mate. Please keep this between us for now."

He glared at me; his cheeks flushed. I could feel his anger all the way to where I was standing. But he was wrong. I wasn't fooling around.

He didn't say anything more. He changed back to his wolf form and ran back in the direction of the house.

I tried to stop him, "Wait Will!" but it was already too late. He was gone. He didn't want to hear it.

I fell to my knees, distraught. This was disastrous! I had hoped so much that my brother would be happy that I had found my mate. The other day, he told me he would love him for sure... Of course, that was before he knew my mate was a vampire... But I had hoped... Tears began crashing down my cheeks.

Damien ran to me and soon enough, I felt his embrace.

"Are you okay, my little wolf?"

Of course, he could see that I wasn't. I know he only tried to be nice and make me feel better.

I shook my head while crying.

"I didn't know how to tell him you were my mate. I didn't want him to find out like that. I wanted to take some time, to let the idea make its way, for him to accept it more easily."

Damien nodded. He understood what I meant. I was a wolf and him a vampire. We were enemies... And yet, we're mates. We were lucky that his brother accepted it easily. But I have no idea how the rest of Damien's friends and family, or mine, will accept the fact that we're mates. I just hoped that it would go better than with Will.

Being in Damien's arms soothed my tears away slowly.

"Who was that? He was with you the other day also. Is he a friend of yours?"

I realized that he has no idea who Will was. I shook my head.

"It was my brother, Will."

Damien looked pensive.

"I guess that explains his size."

I nodded.

"Yes, as the Alpha's son, he's stronger and bigger than other wolves. Like myself ... well, I'm not bigger than other wolves, I took from my mother's side for that, but I'm stronger than other wolves of the pack."

That's the story of my life! As the Alpha's daughter, I was expected to be bigger than the other wolves of the pack. But what can I do? I'm a petite wolf. You can't judge by the size, though. I'm stronger than other wolves. All my life people have misjudged me by my size. I've always liked to prove them wrong.

"You think he's going to be alright?"

I thought for a while, calming myself down, taking a few deep breaths before nodding.

"Yes, I guess I'll have to explain everything to him tomorrow."

I stayed in Damien's arms, just enjoying being with him for the time being. I didn't want to get away from him, even if I had too.

Damien whispered into my ear. "I can barely make it through the day without you, you know."

My heart fluttered at his words. I knew just what he meant!

"Oh Damien, I won't be able to live like that for a long time. My wolf yearns for you all day long. It's unbearable."

If only he knew how much I thought about him every minute of the day.

"I will find a way for us to be together, I promise."

I started kissing his neck, full of hope at his promise. He cupped my face with his hand, bringing our mouths together and kissed me sweetly.

My brother's words kept repeating themselves in my head. All while my sister is still unconscious... It's not that I had forgotten about her. It's just that my thoughts had been busy elsewhere... You know, being hunted, wounded and then trying to heal back.

"Damien, did you go and see the sorcerer? For my sister?"

Damien's gray eyes were staring at me as he smiled.

"Uh-huh, and I made sure he would help, and keep it to himself."

I was so happy!! I only hoped that the sorcerer would find a cure for my sister. I wrapped my hands around his neck and kissed him.

"Thank you so much, my love."

Damien chuckled a little. I loved how sexy his voice sounded.

"It's the least I could do for my mate." He winked.

I stayed in his arms for a few minutes, enjoying his presence, letting his love fill me, enjoying his kisses. But soon, I knew I had to go back home.

I didn't have to say anything to him, he knew it too.

"I promise this is the last time I have to leave you. I will find a solution; I can't go on like that."

His words were filling me with joy. As we said our goodbyes, feeling already lonely, I ran back home.

I didn't meet anyone going back home. I guess Will already told them I was fine. Did he tell them about my mate? Or did he decide to keep it to himself, I wondered?

I was greeted by everyone when I arrived at the house.

"Kate! Where were you?" My parents looked worried.

I guess Will didn't tell them. My eyes fell on him. He was leaning back on the wall, his arms crossed. He was waiting for my answer, like the rest of them.

My mother added, "Will told me he saw you coming back and that you were fine, but we didn't have any details. Please, tell us! I've been worried sick! This is the second time you go missing."

I thought a little and decided to say the truth was the easiest and best thing to do.

"I was in the forest... I went and saw Uncle Zach. But then, as I was about to come home, I was attacked by assassins."

Everyone gasped at my words. Even Will's eyes seemed to soften a little as he watched me.

"I ran for a long time. I got injured, I hit my head and spent the night in a cave... Only today did I heal enough and was able to make my way back home."

Well … okay, almost the truth. I still wasn't ready to speak about Damien being my mate.

"Assassins?" my mother screamed.

My father was raging. I didn't really want to talk further about it. I was hoping no one would ask where I found that pretty dress.

"I'm feeling a little tired…" I lied.

They didn't ask about the dress. No one knew that I had something different on when I went to search for Zach. Well … other than Zach himself. But he didn't seem to notice. Maybe he was so deep into his mind that he didn't remember?

"You rest for today," my father ordered.

I nodded to him. You must do what the Alpha orders anyway. Although this time, I was happy about it, I laughed at myself. We did a group hug.

When everybody was gone and it was only Will and I, he came close to me and asked, "How much of what you just said is true? I didn't find you in a cave…"

I looked at him, he still was doubtful, but his stare was softer.

"Everything is true Will... The only thing I left out was that I encountered my mate's brother. He brought me to my mate and it's my mate that healed me this fast. I just ... didn't want to tell them about my mate yet."

Will took a moment to decide if he wanted to believe me or not. I waited anxiously for him to decide. He was my brother and I wanted him to trust me. After a moment, he spoke.

"We've been through a lot. We've always been there for each other. So, I'll trust you're telling me the truth. And if what you say is really true, then he did save your life..."

I breathed a sigh of relief. I was happy my brother believed me. I smiled at him. He hugged me; it was a brotherly hug that felt good.

"You know it doesn't mean that I trust him, right? I'll never be able to trust a vampire. I don't approve the fact you have a vampire as a mate."

I looked at my brother, I could see in his eyes he was serious. But hey, at least it was a step forward. I couldn't help being glad at least a little bit.

"You know I didn't choose my mate. The moon goddess does."

My brother sighed.

"Yeah, that's the worst in all this story. But hey, you're still my sister."

I couldn't hold a laugh. My brother soon joined too. I was feeling genuinely happy. The battle wasn't won yet, but it was a good start.

I went off to bed and fell asleep immediately, exhausted from my day.

The following morning, when I woke up, my father wanted to see me. He was staring out the window when I came to his study. Sheets of papers were scattered all around his desk like he had searched for something. It wasn't like him to have a cluttered desk, so I wondered what was happening.

"Hey Dad!" I said casually.

He turned around and I could see he was tired. He smiled at me.

"Hey sweetie. I'm so happy to see you."

"You look tired."

He rubbed the back of his neck.

"Yeah, I've been busy. I've been thinking about those assassins that have been chasing you the other day…"

Oh … so he was worried about me. That's not good. I don't want my father to worry about me. What's more, I don't want my father to assign a guard that will follow me everywhere. Or worse, I don't want to be stuck at the pack's house. I know I'm an adult but for werewolves, it doesn't matter. What the Alpha says, everyone obeys…

"I think it's time I talk to you about something."

I had absolutely no idea what he could want to talk about. I listened, curious.

"Years ago, the nymphs were being attacked by a manticore that was roaming their territory."

"A manticore?"

"Yes, a creature with the body of a lion, the head of a human and the tail of a scorpion. It was killing and eating every nymph he could get his hands on. The nymphs were getting decimated very quickly and as much as they fought back, they couldn't kill the evil beast."

I didn't really know where this story led, but it was quite entertaining. I never heard about manticores before. It looked like a creature taken out of a book.

My father seemed pretty serious... I tried to stop thinking and to concentrate.

"The nymphs sought help to defeat the manticore. Our pack's wolves united. We devised an attack plan. We trapped the beast, and when he couldn't move anymore, succeeded into killing it, together with the nymphs."

I looked at him, he was dead serious. I guess he really believed all this story. I didn't really understand why he was telling me all of this.

"Since that day, in order to thank us for what our ancestors did, the nymphs awaken the inner power of our Alpha."

Wait. What?

"The inner power of our Alpha?"

"Yes, my daughter, every Alpha of our pack has an inner power that other werewolves don't have. The nymph's Queen awakens it each generation, as a thank you for the service we have rendered them."

I didn't know what to answer. I just watched, my mouth agape. Does this have anything to do with the "heirloom" the sorcerer was talking about? Was this the power that the vampire lord seeks?

My father continued.

"Usually, we awaken the power when the next Alpha rises to become the leader of the pack... But since you have been chased by assassins. I think it would be best to do the awakening now."

This was so much to take in. I didn't even know where to start.

"What's our inner power like?"

My father shrugged his shoulders.

"It's different for everyone. My father had pacifism powers. That's how he managed to unite so many wolf packs together. As for me, I have a rock skin ability, allowing me for a period of time, to harden my skin to protect myself. It acts as a shield and reduces the damage I receive. It allows me to gain the upper hand in many battles."

I was in shock. How was it that I only learned about all of this? I guess it was true then. I truly have an "heirloom," an inner power hidden inside me. I wondered what it would be for me. "Tonight, is the full moon. You need to go see Ayanna, the Queen of the Melian nymphs. She resides in the sacred grove, to the north. You need to find her tonight."

I nodded to my father. He showed me the sacred grove on my phone. It wasn't very far but I needed to leave now if I wanted to make it before night fall.

I went to prepare myself for the journey ahead. That's when I realized I wouldn't be there to meet Damien. Or if I was, I was going to be late.

I connected to Damien via our mate bond.

"Hey my love."

"What is it, my little wolf?"

"I might be late tonight. I have to go see the nymph Queen."

"The nymph Queen?"

I giggled. I could hear his astonishment even through our mate bond.

"It's a long story. I'll tell you when I get to you."

"Okay. I miss you, my little wolf. I'll see you tonight."

"I miss you too, my love. See you later."

I knew today would be a long day. But I was full of hope. I was still shocked about all that story of inner power and nymph. But hey, it can only help, right? With any luck, this power will help me to stop the war and be able to stay with my mate.

Chapter 13 (Damien)

Memories of the past

It was only morning when Kate told me she would be late tonight. Spending the day without her always felt like I was lost in the ocean and getting to see her at night was the lifeboat that was keeping me going. At least she told me she would be there tonight. I would be patient; I will wait for her.

In the meantime, I went to search for my aunt Lilith. Soon I found her, she was in the war room, studying the strategy for the upcoming war on the werewolves. The thought of the war threatening to start put so much pressure on me. I had to avoid it at all costs. Not only did I want to protect my mate, but I also wanted to protect her friends and family. She would be crushed if everyone she loved would die. This war could not happen.

Lilith looked completely absorbed by the documents she was looking at when I entered the room.

"Aunt Lilith?" She raised her head as I spoke her name, surprised, but then relaxed and smiled when she saw me.

"Damien, it's good to see you."

I didn't know exactly how to approach the subject. It's been such a long time since I've had a real conversation with my aunt. I thought it would be a good idea to spend some time alone with her, maybe she would open up more to me. "Would you like to take a stroll with me?"

She looked pleasantly surprised by my demand.

"Why, it's been such a long time since you've asked me to spend time with you!"

I smiled at her, explaining, "Duties as a prince and heir to the throne can keep me quite busy."

She nodded as she understood what I meant. She then extended her arm, waiting for me to grab it.

We started walking arm in arm, as we did when I was smaller, and we would go spend some time together.

Lilith smiled at me, she looked genuinely happy.

"It's been quite some time since we've done this."

I wanted to add that it's been quite some time since I've seen her that happy, but I preferred to keep it to myself, in case it would darken the mood.

As we walk, I bring her to the garden where she used to take me as a kid. It was a garden framed by very tall trees. A few flower patches here and there always seemed to attract butterflies. In the back of the garden stood the vampire lord's favorite work of arts. On the side of the path stood a few benches where we could sit. It looked exactly how I remember it. It's as if time itself had stopped, preserving this place in a perfect state. For a moment, I felt as if I was a kid again.

I looked at my aunt and surely, she remembered it too, as she looked everywhere with wide eyes and the biggest grin. To top it all, I added with a small voice, "Did you see all the colors of butt-flies auntie?"

She laughed. "Oh Damien! I remember how you couldn't pronounce, 'butterflies.' It was so cute!"

I laughed with her as we sat at one of the benches.

"Yes, and every time, you would correct me and ask me to say, 'butterflies' properly."

I smiled. It was as if it was just yesterday. I could see it clearly in my mind.

Lilith sighed happily. "Thank you so much for bringing me here, Damien! This brings back so many good memories."

"Yes, it does. We used to spend a lot of time together, even as I got older. But all of a sudden, you stopped wanting to spend time with me."

I was speaking of when she started to get invested with the war. After the book was stolen. She knew what I meant. I saw her face darken as I guessed it would. I tried to gain her trust. I hoped she would talk to me if I played innocent.

"Did I do something that made you angry? That made you not want to spend time with me?"

Her eyes widened as she hastily replied, "oh god no! Damien, you've always been the sweetest angel! Don't blame yourself sweetie."

I smiled at her. "You comfort me, I thought I might have done something to upset you."

She smiled back as I spoke.

Now I needed to get her to speak about a potential werewolf lover. Which wouldn't be easy. I wasn't sure exactly how to get her to speak about that. Playing the innocent card seemed to be a good strategy again.

"Hey auntie, can I ask you a question?"

She nodded slightly.

"You know, before all that war talk with the werewolves. Would have it been possible for vampires and werewolves to be friends?"

I decided asking about "friends" would be easier than lovers. I guess I'll just see how she reacts from there. And luckily I didn't ask about the "lovers" part as her face went from smiling to stern. I could see that I've struck a chord.

"Damien, even when the peace treaty had not been broken, werewolves and vampires have always been natural enemies. Werewolves cannot be trusted! Friendship is out of the question!"

I could now see fury in her eyes.

I decided to push my luck a little more. I really wanted to see her reaction if I went further.

"So... I guess being lovers is out of question then?"

Her face went blank. She looked like she had seen a ghost as she fidgeted nervously with her fingers.

"Where did you get a silly idea like that? Of course, this could never happen!"

I shrugged my shoulders and struck the final blow. "I don't know, when I went to kidnap the prisoner the other day, I met a guy that looked friendly. His name was Zach."

I watched as her mouth went agape. She froze and didn't seem to know what to answer.

She turned her face to the side so I couldn't see her whole face anymore. She looked hurt and her voice was trembling. "Whatever you think you saw when you went there, you are mistaken. They cannot be trusted."

Without saying anything more, she got up and walked away, without looking back at me. I didn't try to stop her. I knew she needed the time alone. And it also confirmed that there was something between her and Zach. From her reaction, they were more than just friends. Something happened. I don't know what exactly, but whatever it was, it hurt her, and it still hurts, even today.

I watched her go, feeling sorry for bringing those memories back to her. But in order to solve this puzzle, I had to. I hoped she wouldn't hold a grudge against me.

*********** Kate's POV ***********

I was driving in my car for a while. I passed a river that flew north of the pack's house and passed a mountain. After that it was only corn fields for a while. I listened to the radio until I finally came to a big forest. This was the forest where I would find the nymph's sacred grove.

I parked my car on the side of the road. I would have to do the rest of the journey on foot. It didn't matter. I loved walking into the woods.

It appeared to be a forest of ash trees. Rays of the sun were filtering through the leaves of the trees. Fairies and butterflies could be seen flying through the ferns and flowers. It was a beautiful sight, and I couldn't help feeling peaceful and happy walking through the woods.

The further I went, the taller the trees were. I finally arrived at a very tall tree. It was at least two times taller than other trees. It stood strong and its trunk was so wide, it would take at least four people to go around with their arms. Its branches were full of white and pink flowers. It was the only tree that had flowers and I wondered how it was possible for it to have flowers since we were in summer.

"This tree is always blooming. It's the tree of Life."

I turned my head to see who was speaking. To my side stood a tall woman. Instead of legs, it looked like her lower body was composed of tree roots. The roots came up to her torso. She looked human from the torso up. Roots and leaves went and made her a kind of bikini. She had elf ears but other than that, her face was one of a graceful woman. Finally, her hair was long and composed of vines and lianas with flowers blooming in them. Butterflies seemed to follow her as she walked.

I was taken by her beauty and couldn't find a word to say.

"I was expecting you, Kate. Your father told me you would come."

I was surprised to see she knew my name. That could only mean.

"Are you Ayanna?"

She nodded in acknowledgment.

"I am."

I remembered she was the nymph Queen, so I curtsey to show my respect.

"Your Majesty."

She smiled at me.

"Rise. We have many things to prepare before the sun sets."

I raised myself and followed her.

*********** Damien's POV ************

As I walked back into the castle, I decided to pay a little visit to Elwin and see how his research was going. As usual, when I entered his room, he was busy with some sort of experiment. I wondered if sometimes he did something other than experiments. Did he ever stop to eat? Did he even sleep at night?

I decided I didn't need to look angry or mean to him today. I would wait up and see what he had to say before deciding if I needed extra persuasion.

I spoke his name and he turned himself, without dropping his experiment this time.

He slightly bowed to me. "Ah! My prince! I was hoping you'd come and see me today," he said, looking excited.

He put down his experiment and hastily went to gather something from a shelf.

"I guess this means you had the time to do the task I asked you?" I inquired.

Elwin nodded, "Yes my prince! It was an interesting case! Very interesting!"

I stayed there, waiting for an explanation, as he was searching for something inside a small wooden chest.

"You see, I don't know whose blood it is you brought. It seems this person is under a very powerful curse. I've never seen a magic this powerful before! Even the lord's magic is lesser than this!"

I was taken aback by his last sentence. My father's powers were by far the most powerful and dreaded powers I knew. Everyone obeyed him, careful not to anger him and feel his wrath. What could be more powerful than that, I wondered?

"That's very interesting indeed. Nonetheless, do you have a cure for this magic?"

Elwin vaguely smiled. "I'm not sure, my prince. This is uncharted territory. As such powerful magic has never been seen, it's hard for me to know if I can cure it."

This was not what I wanted to hear, but I couldn't be mad at him for that. If this magic was as powerful as he said it was, then who knew how to dispel it?

Finally, he looked like he had found what he was looking for as he took a flask from the chest before turning back my way.

"I brewed a special potion, made of the strongest reagents I had. If this doesn't work, then it is out of my league, and you'll have to search elsewhere."

He handed me the flask. It contained a strange glowing blue liquid in it. I held it very carefully, looking through it at eye level, in awe. From the effects the healing potion had on Kate, I had great hope this potion would work on her sister. I put the flask in my pocket, thanking Elwin.

As I was about to leave his laboratory, I heard Elwin calling my name.

I turned back as he asked timidly, "My prince... If I dare to ask, are we even now?"

I smiled at his question. It was legitimate. He helped me greatly. I could forgive what he did to Kate the other day, considering the fact he was only following my father's orders.

"Yes, Elwin, we're even."

He looked relieved by my answer. I exited his room. Today was turning out to be a good day, I felt happy.

I was walking back to my room when I bumped into my brother.

"Hey! Are you coming for supper today?"

It's been a few days since I joined my family for supper. I was always locking myself into my room to eat, then leaving early to go meet with Kate. I haven't had a lot to talk about, my thoughts always wandering back to my mate that was away from me.

"I don't know, I have plans tonight."

My brother smirked. "Yes, I've noticed you've been going out at night a lot... I guess I know

287

why." He added with a wink, before continuing. "Mother has been wanting to see you."

I sighed. I loved my mother; I know she must be missing me or wondering what's up with me. She always takes care of me, even though I am grown up.

"I guess I can join supper tonight."

My brother grinned as he patted my back. "That's good to hear!"

We walked together to go eat supper with our family.

As we arrived, my parents were already there, as well as Lilith. She raised her eyes as I entered the room and gave me a big smile. I guess it meant she didn't hold a grudge about earlier. I smiled back at her; I was relieved. I loved my aunt very much and I didn't want her to be mad at me.

My mother stood up as we arrived, and came to embrace me.

"It's been a while since I've seen you, my son. I'm happy that you decided to join us tonight."

I smiled at her. "I've been quite busy lately, sorry."

My father gave me his usual stern look. I ignored him and sat by my brother's side to eat.

The food was great, and everybody was talking but I wasn't listening. The only thing on my mind was Kate. I had to find a way for me to stay with her. I needed her by my side as I needed to breathe.

Being away from her was taking its toll on me. It was eating me inside. I was so lost in my thoughts; I paid no attention to everything going on around me. By the end of the supper, Arius looked at me and asked, "you know, I can tell something's on your mind. Care to share it with me?"

I didn't mind talking to my brother about this. But I couldn't talk to him with all the people around the table. I looked at him, then pointed with my eyes at people around the table. My brother followed my gaze and understood.

We excused ourselves from the table and went to my room, where we could talk away from prying ears.

I closed the door behind us, so we were alone. Arius looked at me. "You haven't talked the entire meal. You didn't even say anything when Dad bragged his usual stories. What's going on?"

I looked at my brother. I thought back at the fact he saved my precious Kate. He was always there for me and for her. I thought about how he lost his mate the most tragic way possible. And yet, here he was again, taking care of me. I felt so close to him right now.

"I can't go on like this, Arius. I need to find a way to stay by Kate's side or I'll go crazy. I miss her so much, it's unbearable!"

I could see Arius's brotherly gaze on me, fully understanding what I meant. My brother sighed, rubbing the back of his head with his hand.

"Hmmm... That's a good problem to solve. But don't worry, it's not like we can't fix it."

I've tried to think so much about this already, but I've found no solutions yet.

"She can't stay here... And I can't stay at her house either. And it's not like I could stay hidden with her in the forest forever either..." I told him.

My brother seemed to ponder a bit. "... Or maybe you could."

I looked at him with questioning eyes. He had a smirk on his face.

"Remember that chalet we used to go with our parents as kids?" he asked me, excited.

I thought back. We used to go on a family vacation in a chalet in the forest at the base of a mountain when I was a kid. It was a beautiful chalet, not that luxurious but it had all the necessary accommodations. I remember how much fun I had with my brother when we went! I don't really know why we stopped going.

"Yeah! Now that you mention it, I remember! We used to go there a few times a year."

My brother nodded. "Do you still remember where it is?"

"How could I forget?"

"You know it's still owned by our parents, right? Which means that right now, it should be empty, waiting for someone to go there."

This was such a great idea; I couldn't even believe it! I jumped at my brother and hugged him, patting him on the back. "You are saving me; you have no idea!"

I was so happy! I felt this huge burst of emotions that wanted to come out. But the first thing that came to my mind is that I needed to tell Kate as soon as possible.

My brother laughed lowly. "Yes, I can understand. I went there to hide with my mate before Father discovered. It's a great hiding place."

I looked at him, surprised but couldn't say a word as my brother. "Don't worry, I'll find an excuse to tell Mom as to why she doesn't see you around for a few days."

I couldn't be happier! How come I didn't think of that?

"Thank you so much Arius! Omg I can't believe this! I can't wait to see Kate's reaction when I tell her that!"

My brother laughed and looked outside at the sky getting dark.

"I guess it's about time you go and tell her, right?"

I laughed too.

"You bet it is! Although, she told me she would be late tonight... But it doesn't matter."

I thanked my brother again as I took my leave to meet with Kate. I had so many things to tell her, I couldn't wait to see her.

************ Kate's POV ************

I watched as the sky darkened. The full moon was slowly rising in the sky. We needed the full moon, said Ayanna. We need my wolf to be at her strongest. I still had no idea what to expect of this.

I sat on the ground, on a stone in the nymph's sacred grove. Fairies were busy arranging flower petals all around me in a circle on the ground. With the sun setting, the fairies began to glow, and a trail of light could be seen everywhere they went. It gave a magical vibe to the air. It was so pretty.

Ayanna came up to me and sat in front of me. Other nymphs sat around us. She put a small glass in front of me, containing a green beverage.

"You will need to drink this cocktail."

I had never drank anything that looked like that before. Suddenly, I began to wonder if this was such a good idea.

"What's in it?"

"It contains many plants and herbs, but most importantly, absinthe."

I gasped.

"Isn't this alcohol illegal?"

She shook her head.

"Maybe in the human countries it is. But not in the realm of nymphs. But don't be afraid my child, there is just a few drops in the drink."

I've heard countless stories about absinthe and wasn't really sure I wanted to try it. I guess that I didn't really have much choice in the matter.

"Absinthe contains a substance that reacts to your inner wolf. That's how we'll be able to awaken your inner power. It has been done this way for generations."

I pondered at what she just said. This meant my father, and his father and all the others before me have always drank this to unleash their full potentials. They all lived through it. It shouldn't be too dangerous then, right?

I nodded to Ayanna.

"I just need to drink this?"

"Yes, and I will guide you through the rest."

I wasn't sure what to expect and was a little nervous. But it was already nighttime. I wanted to get through this and then go see Damien.

Fairies began dancing all around us and the nymphs began a chant in a language I didn't know. I don't know if they used some kind of magic or if it was a special invocation, but my mind went blank, and peace filled me. Without even thinking, I grabbed the drink in my hands.

I brought the glass to my lips, afraid to take the first sip. What would it taste like? Would it be disgusting?

It gave a lemon and spices smell. I took a deep breath and gathered my courage. "This can't be that bad," I thought to myself.

I drank it down in a few sips only, making sure I don't change my mind by going too slow. I realized afterwards that the taste was not bad at all. It tasted like a spicy lemonade. I kind of liked it.

I looked at Ayanna, she was smiling at me.

"Now, my child. I need you to let your wolf take control of you. You need to let her out, but don't change. Just give her control of your human body."

I wasn't sure what she meant. Give my wolf control of my human body? I've never done this in my whole life.

It didn't take long for me to feel the effects of the drink. It started with a fiery feeling inside me, a little bit like when you drink a stiff cocktail. It spread through my whole body slowly. It wasn't hurting or anything, I just felt this warmth everywhere inside of me.

At the same time, I could feel my head starting to turn a little. I felt my wolf getting more restless. She wanted out, she needed out.

I just stayed there, not really knowing what to do.

"Don't fight her. Let her come to me."

I was hearing what Ayanna was saying, but I had no idea how to do so. My body felt heavy, and I couldn't move. I felt this power growing inside of me. It was burning inside, and I needed to let it out, lest I be consumed by it.

At one point, I felt something snap inside of me. I felt my wolf come forward. I felt drawn inside. I saw my hands move, but I wasn't controlling anymore. Now I understood what she meant. I watched, in awe, as my wolf took control of me.

Ayanna smiled.

"You did it, watch the beauty of your wolf."

She took a small mirror from her side and showed me. From inside myself, I saw my reflection in the mirror she was holding. I recognized everything except those two golden eyes staring back at me. Those were my wolf's eyes. Glowing fiercely in the mirror, taking a hold of my human body for the first time.

What will happen to me? I wondered. Will I stay like this forever? I started to panic a little, my breathing quickening.

Ayanna surely picked up on this as she quickly said,

"Calm down, my child. Everything will be fine. We just need to awaken your powers and you'll be able to take back control."

Her words were enough to calm me down.

I still felt this heat burning inside of me and wondered when it would stop.

Ayanna took my hands in hers.

"Tell me, what do you see?"

I didn't see anything. I wondered what she meant when I realized that she was talking to my wolf.

Suddenly, my mind was filled with fire and angels. I realized that my wolf couldn't speak, she didn't know how, so instead, I was seeing what she wanted to answer.

Ayanna was looking intensely at me, as if she could see through my eyes. Could nymphs do such a thing? I wondered.

It all felt so real and overwhelming. At one point, my wolf, or should I say "myself," howled to the moon. It was a howl coming from deep inside of me. After that I blacked out.

When I opened my eyes, I was back in control of my body. My wolf was back inside, as usual. She was fine, she looked like she was happy and at peace. I was lying on the floor.

I raised myself up. Ayanna was still there with me.

"How are you feeling?"

I took a second before answering.

"Fine... I guess."

The fire I felt inside of me was gone. I was feeling at peace. I looked around me, feeling a little disoriented.

"It's okay, you passed out a little. It's normal. Look."

On the ground laid a fiery spear. I wondered where it came from.

"You have a holy fire spear, my dear child."

I wasn't quite sure if I understood right.

"I have what?"

"Your inner power. You can summon a holy fire spear."

I took the spear into my hands, amazed. Did I really make that appear? As I examined the spear, it disappeared.

Ayanna smiled at me.

"Summoned weapons will usually last only a few minutes, but they are very strong. You should use them wisely in battles."

"How will I summon it?"

"Now that your inner power has been awakened, it should be fairly easy. Just think about it and it should appear. Your wolf will know."

"Do I need to let my wolf control my body every time?"

Ayanna shook her head.

"No, now that it is done, you won't have to do that every time you want to use the spear."

Just as I was about to try to summon my holy fire spear, she added.

"Don't overdo it. It takes quite a lot of energy. You should only use it when necessary."

I nodded at her. This was a good advice. I'll try it when I need it then.

I looked at the time. It was already midnight. I really needed to get to Damien. It will take me a few hours to get to him. He must already be waiting for me.

"Thank you very much, Ayanna. I wish I could stay more, but there's a place I really need to be."

She gave me a knowing smile.

"Of course, my child."

I wondered how she could know where I needed to be? Or maybe I was mistaken, and she didn't know. At this moment, it didn't matter. All that was important was that I get to Damien.

"I'm coming, my love," I pushed through his mind, before getting into my car.

Chapter 14 (Damien)

Amnesia

I was so eager to see Kate. I arrived at the lake before her. I knew she would be late, but I couldn't help myself. I missed her so much!

Tonight, the lake was covered with a thin layer of mist. The fog extended to the surroundings, making it look like I was in this eerie dream. But I knew this was not a dream and I couldn't wait for my love to come and meet me. I listened to the frogs singing and watched as the stars shone like diamonds in the sky.

I've been waiting for a while. I was getting impatient, but I would wait as long as I needed to.

Finally, I saw someone walking through the fog, coming to me. I knew who it was. I could smell her sweet heavenly scent from where I was, guessing her curves in the mist. Finally, she was near enough that I could see her bewitching smile.

"Finally," I purred in a husky voice.

Kate looked at me, I could read desire in her eyes. "I missed you so much!" she whispered as I embraced her, feeling her body against mine.

Having her in my arms after spending the day without her felt so good. I kissed her tenderly, sliding my tongue in her mouth as she parted her lips. She tasted like paradise. I felt her heart beat faster as I slid my finger through her hair. She let out a moan when I caressed her back and grabbed her hips. She roamed my chest with her hands, feeling my muscles. I groaned a little, this moment was just perfect. We stayed like that for a moment, cherishing our reunion, basking in each other's love.

I finally broke the kiss and held her close to me.

"You were pretty late today," I teased her.

"I know. I went to see Ayanna."

"Ayanna?"

I had no idea who this Ayanna was. Kate giggled.

"It's the Melian nymph's Queen."

Still had no idea who this was but at least I had an explanation.

"And what did you do with this Ayanna?"

"Well… Remember when your sorcerer said I had an heirloom inside of me? It turns out it was true."

I tried to find something to answer, but I didn't find anything. I couldn't believe Elwin was right about that. I didn't really want it to be true. Only more reasons for my father to try to chase the woman I loved.

"Why didn't you tell me about it?"

She looked sorry as she spoke.

"Well, I only just did find out. I didn't know about it."

I stroked her cheek gently with the back of my hand.

"My father told me everything this morning. Ayanna, she helped me to awake my inner power. I didn't even know I had it. You have to believe me, Damien."

She looked like she was trying to convince me so hard, but she didn't have to.

"Hey, calm down, my little wolf. I believe you. I'll always will."

She smiled at my words. It made her look irresistible. I kissed her sweet lips.

"So, what's this inner power then?"

"It turns out I can summon a holy fire spear!"

"What?"

I watched Kate's eyes sparkle with excitement as she looked at me. That inner power was amazing. And it could prove very useful to my father in the war.

"Does that mean everyone in your family can do that?"

Kate shook her head.

"No, it's different for everyone."

That was pretty interesting but also quite scary. I didn't want anyone to know about this. I didn't want my dad to find out. I wanted Kate to be safe.

"Kate this is amazing! You will keep it a secret, right?"

"Why?"

"Well, I wouldn't want anyone, especially not my dad, to come after you in order to gain that power."

She thought for a moment.

"Huh… I didn't think of it that way. But now that you mention it, it makes sense. Thanks, my love. I'll be careful."

I smiled, reassured that she would at least keep that in mind. I also had lots of things to tell her as well and I was eager to do so.

"Hey, my little wolf, I have something for you. You're going to be happy."

Kate looked at me with the cutest smile on her face.

I handed out the flask that Elwin gave me. In the dark of the night, it was glowing even more. Kate looked at it with intrigued eyes.

"That is for your sister."

Her eyes lightened up. "Really?"

"Uh-huh. Elwin wasn't able to find out exactly what happened to her. But one thing is for sure; the magic that's holding her unconscious, is stronger than the vampire's lord magic."

Kate looked shocked at those last words. She hesitated, then asked, "… Does it mean that there's no way a vampire did this to her?"

I nodded. "It would be very unlikely, since the vampire lord is the strongest of all vampires."

She seemed relieved by my answer.

"Our sorcerer was not sure this would cure her, but it's the strongest potion he could make. If it doesn't work, then we need to find another solution to help your sister."

Kate looked like she was keen to try the potion on her sister. I could see her eyes burning with anticipation. She looked so impatient that I was wondering if she was going to go see her right away. Which I wouldn't allow since I still wanted to hold her in my arms and had lots of things to tell her.

She was so cute it made me laugh a little. I grabbed her hand gently, asking her softly, "you're not leaving me already, are you?"

She blushed a little as I kissed the top of her hand. "Of course not!"

I smiled, happy with her answer. "Good, because I have another important thing, I want to tell you."

"Really? What is it?" she asked with a playful look. At this moment, all I wanted to do was kiss her.

"God you are so pretty! I just want to treasure you forever," I whispered.

She giggled. "That's the important thing you wanted to tell me?" she asked with a wink.

I realized I had spoken my thoughts out loud and smirked at her. "Well, it's pretty important too... But I had something else to tell you as well."

I made her wait for a few seconds before talking. I could see she was getting impatient, which made me want to tease her even more. But I didn't wait for too long before telling her.

"I went to see my aunt Lilith today."

Kate's eyes widened as I spoke, she knew where I was going with my story and was eager to hear it.

"I asked her if it were possible for werewolves and vampires to be lovers, but she told me werewolves could never be trusted."

Kate's eyes turned to the ground as I said that. I could feel she was sad through our mate bond. I squeezed her hand and raised her chin with my fingers so she would look me in the eyes. "Hey, my aunt said that. It doesn't mean that I agree with her, aright?"

Then to remind her, furthermore, how much I loved her, I tilted my head and pushed my hair to the side so she could clearly see my neck, exposing the mark she gave me. One look is all it took to remove all of her sadness and make her smile again. She grazed against the skin of my neck with her fingers, sending shivers all over my body as she passed over the mark on my neck.

"You're right, I almost forgot," she told me.

I asked, perplex, "how could you almost forget that you're my mate? It's kind of important!"

She giggled a little, "I'm just playing with you. I would never forget. My wolf yearns for you all day long."

A purr of satisfaction came out of my chest as I heard those words, relieved. I needed her by my side more than ever.

"As I was saying, Lilith had a strong reaction when I talked about werewolves and vampires being lovers. So, to test the waters a little, I told her that I've met a werewolf that looked friendly, and that his name was Zach... You should have seen her reaction. She looked hurt; her voice was trembling. I don't know exactly what happened between them, but she definitely knows him."

Kate was still thinking about all that I've just said, when a noise came from the bushes.

"Maybe I can help clarify," a man's voice said.

I stood in front of Kate, preparing myself to protect her against whoever might be there. My nails were already growing, and my fangs were coming out. I wouldn't let anything happen to my mate.

A man slowly came out of the bushes. He had blond hair and blue eyes, he was tall and looked like he was in good shape, older than Kate. He

311

came out, not showing any signs of aggressiveness.

He looked at me and spoke gently, "Relax, I'm not here to fight with you."

I relaxed a little and shrank back my nails and fangs.

Kate shouted, "Uncle Zach, what are you doing here?"

Huh, so that's Zach, I thought to myself. This ought to be interesting.

Zach was rubbing the back of his neck, searching for an answer. "... I guess, doing the same thing you used to do when you were little," he said while looking at Kate.

Kate smiled at his answer.

Kate looked at me, then said to her uncle, "Zach, this is Damien. He's the one who returned me home a few days ago... And ... well... He's my mate!"

She blushed a little at those last words.

Zach laughed a little, "yeah, that's what I understood from your little conversation."

I asked him, "what have you heard?"

He smiled. "All of it."

Luckily, things didn't get too hot between Kate and me with him watching, I thought to myself. I went by Kate's side and put my arm affectionately around her waist. Kate leaned her head on my shoulder as I heard a soft purr coming out of her chest that made my heart feel warmth.

Zach chuckled quietly as he watched us. "Don't worry. The moon goddess chose you as her mate. As long as she's happy with you, I don't care one bit that her mate is a vampire."

I felt Kate relax at those words. I was happy too. The last thing I wanted was to fight with her family because of our love. All I wanted was for her family to approve of us so we could live together freely.

Zach continued, "besides, although I never completed the mating bond, as you two seemed to have," he winked as he said that, staring at the mark on my neck.

I couldn't help but have a proud look on my face as I knew how important this was for werewolves.

He then spoke more softly, "... My mate is also a vampire..."

Kate put her hands on her mouth as she gasped in surprise.

I guess it all made sense now. I didn't need all the details; Lilith was Zach's mate. That explains how they know each other, and why Kate said they were lovers. Although it didn't explain what happened between them.

"Why are you not by her side then? Why is she so eager to wage war against werewolves?" I asked him.

Zach looked sad. "I only remembered it today... I don't know how I could have forgotten something that important..."

He looked at Kate. "All that talking with you. When you asked me about mates. And when you asked me if I knew a vampire named Lilith. I kept searching, my mind feeling fuzzy. But suddenly I remembered."

That's the weirdest thing I've ever heard. I mean, the mate bond is the strongest thing there is. I know in my heart I could never ever forget that

Kate is my mate. All of me is craving for her all the time.

Kate pushed through our minds, "I could never forget you."

I looked at her and could see passion in her eyes. I squeezed her waist and kissed her softly on the neck.

Kate spoke softly to her uncle, "I don't understand how you could have forgotten about your mate."

He shrugged his shoulders. "I really don't understand it either..."

Then I thought of something that might explain it. But first, I needed to check if he was related to the disappearance of the vampire's book of secrets, eighteen years ago.

I asked him, "That night. Kate told me she saw Lilith give you something. What was it?"

Zach looked at me tensed. "It was the secret books of vampires. The one that holds every secret known about vampires and their history."

Now we were going somewhere! And it could maybe explain how he could forget about his mate.

I asked him, "did you open the book?"

He looked at me. "Well, of course, I opened it!"

"Then this might explain why you forgot about your mate."

Kate and Zach were looking at me with inquisitive eyes.

I explained myself. "The book of vampires is protected by a curse. No one really knows what that curse is. But what if, that curse is one that makes you forget everything? It could explain what happened to you. And it would be an effective curse to make sure to preserve the secrets of the vampires, wouldn't it?"

They both pondered at what I just said and looked like they agreed with me.

"It does make sense," Zach mumbled.

"What did you want to do with the book anyway?" I asked him.

Zach sighed, "I wanted to find a way to expand my lifespan, so I could be able to live forever with Lilith."

He looked sad when talking about that. His goal was of the purest intentions. This curse was so cruel upon him. He only wanted to spend all his life with his mate and to live as long as she would; yet he completely forgot about her.

And to think how Lilith must have suffered from this! The pain and sadness to have your mate, your other half, the one chosen by fate, ripped away from you. She probably thought he didn't love her anymore. But since he didn't refuse her as his mate, that means the mate bond must have never been completely gone. So, she must have yearned for him for years, but never could get reunited with him. That must have been unbearable.

This probably explains what happened a few years ago when my aunt suddenly changed. And why she was so eager to go to war with the werewolves... It also explains why she said werewolves couldn't be trusted. If only I had known, maybe I could've helped her in some way.

"We'll find how to expand my lifespan, and then we'll tell you!" Kate said with determination in her eyes. My sweet Kate. Always this determination and fire inside that I like so much.

"Right, we also need to find a way to expand Kate's lifespan," I added.

Zach smiled at us as he nodded.

But something still puzzled me. Everybody said the werewolves stole the book from us. If Lilith brought the book to him, why does everybody think werewolves stole it?

I asked Zach, "I don't get it. Vampires think werewolves stole the book eighteen years ago. But if Lilith brought it to you, I don't see why they would think that."

"I guess I know the answer to that… When Lilith brought me the book, no one knew she had taken it. It was our secret as we couldn't tell anyone we were mates… The goal was for me to find a way to expand my lifespan, and after it was done, return the book and run away with Lilith. Live far away. A place where no one would question the fact I was a werewolf and that she was a vampire."

This looked like a good solution. But I didn't want to run away. I wanted to find a way for people to approve of our relationship. I was the heir to the throne. Worst-case scenario, I would wait until I became the Lord and make a public statement allowing people to love whoever they wanted. But I was hoping I wouldn't have to wait so long. And I intended to be with Kate starting today as I couldn't stand being apart from her.

Zach continued, "I was supposed to meet her back here one week later and give back the book to her. But as soon as I opened the book, I forgot everything. Or at least, that's the best possible explanation."

Kate spoke softly, "I guess she had to find an excuse for the missing book when people realized it was missing..."

I guess she thought he didn't love her and tricked her in order to get the book, I thought to myself, but decided not to say it out loud, as all of this was probably already hard enough on Zach.

Zach replied, "it makes sense, as this book is of utmost importance to the vampires and under strict surveillance."

"Zach..." I started, "a terrible war is about to break because of this missing book. If you could please return it to me, maybe I could prevent this war from happening."

Zach looked at me, embarrassed. "The thing is... I don't remember where the book is."

I looked at him, surprised.

He explained, "I remember opening it, but I don't know what I did with it afterwards."

"Do you think maybe you could have put it in the library?" asked Kate.

Zach shook his head. "No, this book is quite large and emits a strange magic aura. Somebody would have found it already if it had been in the library."

I was feeling disheartened. It was the one thing we needed to prevent the war. We seemed so close to finding it! But then, it seems we're back at square one. Kate must have felt my feelings through our mate bond as she squeezed me and pushed through my mind, "don't give up, my love."

Those words were all that I needed to bring back the fire in me. "You're right, my little wolf," I pushed through her mind.

"Please Zach, you have to try to remember, you have to try to find it. If this war happens... Kate could be hurt. Her family and friends could be hurt too. I don't want any casualties on either side."

Zach nodded. "Yes, I understand. I will try my best to find it, and to bring it back. It would be for the best if we could avoid this war… Plus, I need to see Lilith."

Of course, he needed. I just didn't know how she would react after all those years. But that was something they had to deal with on their own.

Zach continued, "I guess I should get going then. I have a book to find and a mate to get back to."

Kate nodded, "I guess I should get going too."

I shook my head, holding her arm to keep her with me. "No wait! Not yet, I… I can't continue like that. Please stay with me."

She looked at me. "Aww my love, I know. I want to stay with you too. But you know I have to go back home, and so do you." She had tenderness in her eyes, and I knew she was sad about leaving, but she didn't know what I was about to tell her.

I looked at her with playful eyes. "Actually, I don't."

Kate looked at me with doubting eyes. I loved that look she was making. I liked to toy with her.

"There's a chalet nearby, owned by my family. There is no one there. Please! Come with me. We can stay there together! We don't have to stay apart all day long."

I was feeling all the excitement she was feeling through our mate bond. I could hear her heartbeat speeding up and read the joy on her face. She was so beautiful smiling like that, she could make the diamonds feel jealous.

"Oh Damien! This is a great idea!"

Kate jumped in my arms, hugging me tightly. I put my head in the crook of her neck and enjoyed her sweet scent. But suddenly she took a step back and her face changed from excited to sad. "... But I can't... I mean, my family is going to be worried about me... And I still have to get to my sister and wake her up... And we need to find the book and stop the war ... and..."

I could feel so much doubt in her at this moment. She was trying to take all the problems of the world on her shoulders, and it was way too much. She needed to let others help her out too. I'm her mate, I want to share the burden with her, I want to be able to help her.

I interrupted her, "hey, my little wolf, calm down. This is all too much for one person to handle. Let us help you with this, okay? You know you can count on me. I'm your mate, I'm here for you. Please let me help you."

Zach, who had watched the whole scene, added, "let me handle the book. I was the one who lost it. I'll be the one to find it and bring it back, okay?"

Kate nodded; she calmed a little as we spoke to her.

Then Zach added, "I think you should go to the chalet with Damien. I'll tell your parents that I've asked you to deal with some matter I have with the neighboring wolf pack. That way they'll know you'll be gone for a few days."

An excited Kate asked, "Really. You would do that for me?"

Zach nodded, but then Kate added, "But, I really want to try to wake up Bianca first. And I need to get some of my stuff too."

She looked at me and I could see that when she set her mind to something, nothing could stop her.

"Would it be okay if I come and join you tomorrow morning instead?"

She had those cute puppy eyes; it was impossible to resist. I laughed softly, "of course it is, my little wolf. Let me show you where it is on your phone."

I showed Kate the chalet's location on her phone. That way she was sure not to get lost. Zach looked at the map and said, "oh yeah! I know where this is. It's a nice spot, you're going to enjoy it."

I smiled. He was right, I was going to enjoy this, I thought to myself. Even more than he thought. It's not the location or even the chalet itself that I was looking forward to. I was going to finally spend time alone with my beautiful Kate, all day and all night long. *That's* really what I was looking for.

As we said goodbyes for the night, I gave Zach a friendly pat on the back. It was nice to know I had an ally in Kate's family. My first werewolf ally, I thought to myself.

As Kate came close to me, I could feel the warmth of her breath on my neck. She was so tempting; I couldn't wait for us to be alone.

I whispered to her.

"I'll get the chalet nice and cozy. I'll be there, waiting for you. Please don't make me wait too long, my love."

Kate raised herself on her tiptoes to kiss me as I held her by the waist. I didn't need anything but her to make me happy. I would follow her to the end of the world.

"I'll make it quick; I promise. You'll see, in no time, I'll be back in your arms."

Her words were soothing. The promise of having her to myself all day long woke up a fire inside me I didn't even know existed. I kissed her with passion, barely resisting the urge to take her, right now. I needed her more than ever. I knew she needed to get back to her family tonight and I knew her uncle was still there watching us. But right now, it's as if my heart had taken control of my head. The mate bond pulling me to her more than ever. Making it impossible to resist.

Kate whispered to me, breathless, between kisses, "we'll have all the time we need tomorrow, my love. I need to leave for the night now."

It seems her words were all it took to let my mind gain back control. I guess she had that power over me now.

"You are right. Go, my little wolf, so you can come back to me as soon as possible." I winked at her and let her go. I watched her as she went back towards her family's home with Zach.

I was feeling happy, as I knew this time, she would join me in the morning instead of having to wait a whole day. I made my way to the chalet, with a light heart, thinking about all I wanted to prepare before Kate would arrive tomorrow.

Chapter 15 (Kate)

The demon's curse

As I walked back home with Uncle Zach, I was happier than ever, knowing that I could go see my mate tomorrow and would get to stay with him. My wolf wasn't happy, she wanted to go right now. But I repeated to her, we need to go see my sister first. That was more important.

As we approached the house, Zach told me, "I'm really happy you found your mate. Take good care of him. Don't do as I did."

It must have been so hard on her… But what happened wasn't exactly his fault either.

"You didn't do it on purpose to forget about her… I'm sure you'll be able to repair what was broken."

Zach looked concerned. "… I'm not so sure about that. But I do hope I'll be able to."

We arrived at the house. "You'd better go see if you can get your sister to wake up. I'll try to see if I can recall where I put the book of vampires' secrets."

I nodded at him; he was right. I was tired already, but my sister was more important than sleeping right now.

I entered the house quietly; a lot of people were already sleeping. I entered Bianca's room. As always, Steven was there, sleeping on the chair, leaning on Bianca's bed. I walked slowly to him and gently pat his arm.

I spoke gently, "Steven."

He raised his head, half-opening his eyes.

"Huh?" looking around, he turned his head my way. "Oh, hey Kate. What are you doing here at this hour?"

I smiled at him as I got the vial out for him to see. "I have something to show you."

His eyes widened as he looked at the glowing liquid. "Wow! … What is it?"

"That is something to try to wake up Bianca."

Steven looked at me with a grin on his face. "Really?"

I nodded at him as I walked up to Bianca. "Help me and get her in a sitting position so I can make her drink this."

Steven did as I asked and held Bianca in a sitting position. He held her with great care, tenderness showing in his movements. I could see how much he loved her.

I opened her mouth and tilted her head back a little as I poured the contents of the vial. When she swallowed it all, Steven got her back to her sleeping position gently, as if holding the most precious thing in the world.

We waited a little, but nothing happened.

Steven looked at me. "Is it supposed to work right away?"

I shrugged my shoulders. "I don't know. All I know is that she is afflicted by a very powerful magic or curse. This was the most powerful concoction known, supposed to make her wake up."

I looked at my sister. She looked like sleeping beauty. Maybe a kiss from her lover would wake her up? I laughed at my thoughts.

Steven said, "well, thanks for trying anyways. We'll see if she wakes up eventually."

I gave him a hug. "Yes, sorry she didn't wake right away. I hope she wakes up soon. In the meantime, I'll get some sleep."

Steven nodded. "Yeah, I'll get some sleep too," he said as he got back into the chair.

I went to my room. I was feeling exhausted and fell asleep right away. I had nightmares all night long. I was being chased by something; I could feel its warm breath as it came closer. Every time I woke up, I would fall back asleep and have the same nightmare over again.

At one time I woke up and heard Damien's worried voice in my head asking, "are you alright, my little wolf?"

I guess he felt my fear through our mate bond. I reassured him, "yes, only nightmares, don't worry."

I felt his voice relax. "Okay, I'll make sure you have no nightmares tomorrow when you sleep in my arms."

The thought of sleeping in his arms sounded so great right now! How I wish I could be in his arms, sensing his cool body against mine, surrounded by his scent, feeling loved and protected.

"I miss you," I pushed through his mind.

Soon Damien pushed memories of him hugging me through my mind, making me relax. "Soon my little wolf, we'll be together."

After that I was finally able to get to sleep. I woke up to a scream. It felt like I'd been asleep for a few minutes only but when I looked around, it seemed the sun was already up.

I sat in my bed, trying to get my thoughts together, when I heard the scream again.

I rushed out of my room to stumble on my brother Will, running to Bianca's room. I hadn't spoken to him yet since the other day about my mate. I wasn't sure where he stood at this point. I knew I needed to talk to him before going to the chalet with Damien.

But first things first, I need to see what's going on with Bianca first.

I entered Bianca's room with Will, to find Bianca awake! It was Steven that was screaming. He looked at me, tears of joy on his cheeks.

"Oh my god Kate! It worked!!! You did it! You awoke her!"

Will looked at me with questioning eyes. I didn't have time to answer before Zach barged into the room. He looked at Steven and then at Bianca before he exclaimed himself, "Oh My god Bianca! You're awake! It worked, Kate!"

Once again, Will looked at me. "Would someone please explain why everyone says it's thanks to Kate that Bianca woke up?"

Bianca looked around the room. "Mom and dad are not there?"

Zach shook his head. "No, they are out on a trip to make preparations for the war."

I was so relieved my sister was back with us. I wanted to hug her, but Steven kept her to himself, not letting anyone separate them. "Can I hug my sister?" I asked him with a smile.

I heard his wolf growl a little but he reluctantly let go of her so I could hug her.

"I'm so happy you're back," I told my sister as I hugged her.

"I'm happy to be back … and it seems I have you to thank."

I refrain myself from laughing as I saw my brother's annoyed face. He was the only one who had no idea I had done something to try to cure Bianca.

"I had help from my mate," I started.

Will's face darkened at those words. He knew my mate was a vampire.

Bianca's eyes widened as she shouted in excitement, "You found your mate?"

I giggled at her question.

"Yes, I did, and when you wouldn't wake up, I asked him to help me. He went to see a sorcerer

334

and asked him for help. Yesterday, he gave me a vial of a strong concoction and with Steven's help, I made you drink it."

Zach was smiling, he was there when Damien gave me the vial, so he knew the story already. Bianca and Steven looked amazed.

Will still didn't seem happy.

"So, I guess it took a vampire to break a vampire's curse," he spatt out, angry.

Steven gasped. I shouted back at Will, "Vampires didn't put this curse on Bianca!"

"Oh yeah?" he asked, "How can you be so sure?"

"Because she was cursed by a magic more powerful than the vampire lord's magic!"

Will still didn't believe me, and it was showing on his face.

"Bullshit! Why would you even believe him? He's a vampire!"

I replied softly, "because he is my mate, Will. I know he speaks the truth."

I had no better reason, I could feel it in my heart. If only I could make Will feel what I feel, he would know it's the truth.

But he still didn't believe me. It showed on his face.

Bianca spoke, "she's telling the truth."

All eyes fell on her as she continued.

"While it may have looked like I was asleep, I wasn't. My soul was kept imprisoned by a demon named Eurynomos."

I had never heard of that demon's name, but judging by Zach's face, he knew something about it.

Zach spoke. "Eurynomos… He had been sealed in a sepulcher by the moon goddess herself a very long time ago. But a few years ago, before you were born, some wolves tried to resurrect him. In the end, it was your parents, Sam and Sarah, who defeated him."

I was so surprised; I didn't know what to say. I had never heard of that story before! I looked up to Will and Bianca and they looked as surprised as I was.

"Your mother was taken prisoner by those crazy wolves, but your father rescued her. I was there, we were fighting together. In the end, Sam was wounded, and it was Sarah that fought them off. It turns out she was the moon goddess's daughter."

I just didn't know what to say. I always thought my mother was only human.

Bianca gasped. "That's what he said!"

We all looked at her with questioning eyes.

She explained, "Eurynomos, he kept saying that I was the moon goddess's daughter. That he put a curse on my lineage, even before I was born. And now that I had found my mate, the curse had been activated."

We all looked at her in amazement. She would be the moon goddess's daughter? I guess it could explain why she didn't have the same genes as us. But something didn't make sense!

"If you are the moon goddess's daughter, then why don't you share the same genes as our mother? Our mother was also the moon goddess's daughter, was she not?" I asked, perplexed.

Silence fell upon us as nobody really knew what to answer to my question.

All of a sudden, Zach cried out, "I think I know why!"

We all looked at him, waiting for an explanation.

"After Bianca was born, your mother's power seemed to have disappeared. I've always heard the moon goddess only has one daughter. Maybe, that day, your mother's powers were passed on to you. And maybe the moon goddess's genes were transferred at the same time."

It was a stretch. It's not like I had a better explanation. It's just that it seemed all too far-fetched to be true.

"Either way," I started, "you've known Steven was your mate for a long time, right?" I asked Bianca.

She nodded at me. "Yes, I knew Steven was my mate when I turned eighteen. But he was too young. He couldn't have known it too, so I was patient, waiting for him to get older."

I continued. "So, why would the curse awaken just now?"

Bianca replied, "well, since Steven was too young, the mate bond couldn't activate. But when he turned eighteen, he found out he was my mate

338

too, and the mate bond finally activated. I guess that's what activated the curse."

"Huh," Will said, "I guess it does make sense … kind of…"

We all had that baffled expression on our faces.

"Well, I'm glad that you are fine now," I told Bianca.

She shook her head.

"Well, I'm not totally fine," she explained. "You see, part of my soul is still being held hostage by Eurynomos… As long as he keeps this part of my soul, he will be able to see and hear everything that I do. As I am able to see and hear everything that he does as well."

Gosh this didn't seem to end!

Steven asked, "how can I save you? Please! There must be a way! I need you by my side. I'm your mate, I'll do whatever it takes to save you!"

He looked desperate. It was evident he would go to the end of the world to save her.

Bianca thought for a minute. "I've heard Eurynomos say it was impossible for me to be freed, as it would need for two age-old enemies to associate with each other, and that could never happen."

Zach pondered. "Do you think he meant werewolves and vampires?"

Steven whispered, "of course he must mean us and vampires…"

Will had a stern look on his face, not saying anything. He was leaning against the wall with his arms crossed.

"But it doesn't matter, right? Because your mate is a vampire, so we'll be able to break the curse, right?" Steven asked me, full of hope.

Everybody's hope was lying on my shoulders. I felt a lot of pressure. I thought about Will, who still didn't look like he approved of my mate.

I started, uneasy, not wanting to crush everyone's dream.

"It's not as easy as that… Not everyone will accept Damien with welcoming arms, even if he's my mate. With him being a vampire … a lot of people will not agree with our love."

Steven immediately replied, "he helped to bring my mate back to me, I don't care if he's a vampire. I love him already."

I smiled at him, but I replied, "and yet, my own brother still doesn't accept him. Making peace between us and vampires is not an easy task."

Everybody turned to look at Will, who was still lying against the wall. Will stared at me looking in my eyes, lost in his thoughts. Everybody was waiting on him to say something.

He finally sighed and spoke.
"Listen, I don't like the fact he's a vampire. But he did help us out … and probably saved your life as well… I can't do anything about the fact the moon goddess chose a vampire for your mate… So, I'll give him a chance."

I loved my brother so much. I knew he was making a big effort right now. I hugged him tight, tears of joy falling as I whispered, "thanks little brother, I love you."

He hugged me back. We stayed a few seconds like that before breaking the hug.

"See? All hope is not lost," said Bianca with a smile.

"Don't forget a war is about to break in a few days..." Will started, "mom and dad are out there getting last preparation details ready. I wouldn't get my hopes too high."

"We're going to stop the war," I cried. They all looked at me as I explained myself.

"Damien and I, we want to stop the war. We don't want any casualties."

Zach added, "I will try to help them too. As you see, I haven't told you but ... my mate is also a vampire."

Will, Bianca and Steven gasped.

Bianca replied, "then there is hope!"

I smiled at her. "It's still a long shot, but we're going to try our hardest to bring peace between werewolves and vampires."

"Then I'll help too!" Steven said, with Bianca following soon after, "and so will I!"

But then Will retorted, "you can't."

"And why is that?" she asked him defiantly.

"Because you are still bounded to Eurynomos, and until you are freed from him, he will know our every move if you help us," Will replied.

I have to admit he was right. Although I wished Bianca could help, it was true that Eurynomos would likely try to prevent us from stopping the war if he could. So, it was best if she didn't know too many details about what we were doing. The same goes for Steven since he was her mate.

"I guess it's best if you and Steven don't know too much stuff about us stopping the war," I started. "But it doesn't mean you can't help at all."

Steven asked Will, "I've always had your back when we were fighting together with the pack. Will you have my back this time and help stop this war?"

Will came up to Steven and gave him a fist bump. "Of course, I have your back bro. I'll help prevent this war, and luckily, we'll free my sister from this curse."

He added, "you'd better take good care of your mate. She's my sister so you'll hear from me if you don't."

Steven laughed at his last statement.

"Then it's settled," I started, "I need to pack my things and prepare to leave."

Will asked, perplexed, "leave"?

Oh, that's right! I haven't told them yet.

"I'm leaving for a few days; I'm going to join Damien at a chalet in the woods."

"Mom and dad will never accept this," Will replied.

"That's why you won't tell them where she really is... Officially, she is taking care of stuff with the neighboring wolf pack," Zach said.

Everybody nodded at him, and I felt happy knowing I would be able to go to my mate, as my wolf yearned.

"I'll show you guys where it is, so if you ever need to find me, you'll be able to," I added, getting my phone out to show them where it is on the map.

Just before I left the room, Will grabbed me gently by the arm and took me apart from the others.

"Hey, sorry it started on the wrong foot with your mate. Tell him I bear no grudge against him. And please, keep me updated as to how I can help you stop this war."

I felt so happy that Will decided to accept my mate even if he was a vampire. And more even so since he wanted to stop the war.

"Sure, I'll do that! Thanks, Will," I told him as I hugged him.

I went to my room. I felt like I was walking on a cloud. It's been a long time since I've felt that happy. Things were finally looking like they were getting better. My sister was awake, not fully free but still. We had more allies to try to stop the war. And now was the time to prepare and see my mate. I couldn't wait to go!

I prepared my things to go to the chalet. I took the bare minimum with me and stuck them into a little bag I liked to carry with me. It was lightweight and not too big so I could carry it even when I was in my wolf form without too much struggle.

As I stepped out of the house, Will, Zach, Bianca and Steven came to hug me before I went to the chalet. I looked at them and a warmth filled my

345

heart. It was true we were wolves and that we took care of each other in the pack. But right now, with our common goal of stopping the war, it felt like this was even more. I couldn't have hoped to have that many allies. Together, with Damien, we were a strong team. A glimmer of hope lightened my heart as I said my goodbyes to them as I left.

I took a few steps into the woods, away from prying eyes. Inside, I could feel my wolf calling. She was repeating the same thing over and over again: mate. She wanted out, she wanted to get to him. And now that I was hidden, I took off my clothes, put them in my bag. I let her take control of me. I knew what she wanted. I slowly let the change come. I've always enjoyed the feeling of shifting to my wolf form. Especially when it was not forced, like for a fight or to defend myself, but when it was for pleasure, like today.

It felt relaxing, like slipping into a warm bath. I could feel all my senses heighten so much more than when I'm in my human form. Suddenly, I became aware of the wind breaking through the trees and through my fur. The sweet scent of the dew on the grass hit my nose. I watched as two chipmunks were chasing each other in the leaves, as the thought crossed my mind that they wouldn't make a decent meal.

I could feel my animal instinct take a hold of me. All I wanted to do right now was to get to my mate. I grabbed my bag and started to run through the woods, letting my senses guide me. I could still smell Damien's scent, even though faintly, and follow him to the chalet.

If I had to describe what it meant to be free, I would say it was that. Being able to run freely through the forest, connected to nature, feeling the warmth of the sun on my fur, simply enjoying life.

I ran for some time, not sure for how long, as I didn't care about time right now. I crossed the river that flows into the Sleeping Lake. I climbed a small cliff. I knew I was getting closer as Damien's scent was becoming stronger. This honey and musk scent of his was driving me crazy and I couldn't think about anything else at this moment.

Finally, I saw a big house take shape on the horizon. It wasn't the shabby kind of chalet. It had two floors, with a long balcony on the second floor. In the yard was a spa and a big patio with everything, you would need to host a reception. I asked myself if I was at the right place but sure enough, I could smell my mate's scent. I couldn't wait to see what the interior looked like.

I pushed through Damien's mind, "I'm here, come outside."

It didn't take much time before Damien came outside. He had tied his hair in a low bun, and I thought it looked even sexier that way. He was wearing jeans and a tight shirt. I watched him as he searched for me, not knowing I would be in my wolf form. I could have told him through our mate bond, but it was funnier to wait and see what his reaction would be when he would see me.

Chapter 16 (Damien)

Reunited

I was sitting on the couch, relaxing, when I heard Kate called for me.

"I'm here, come outside."

I had been waiting for those words all morning and now she was finally here! I sprang to my feet and went outside.

I looked out but Kate was nowhere to be found. Did she go to the wrong chalet? She just told me she was there so surely; she must have arrived at *some* chalet. How could she go to the wrong place? I showed her on her phone.

I pushed through her mind, "Where are you? I'm outside and I don't see you."

Just as I pushed that in her mind, I saw a small gray wolf slowly coming out of a bush. The wolf stared at me and surely, I recognized her right away. There she was, looking at me with her deep hazel eyes.

"There you are my little wolf."

I told her out loud, smiling at her. Be it in wolf form or in human form, she was breathtaking.

She approached me and I grabbed the bag she was carrying. She rubbed her muzzle tenderly against me as I passed my fingers through her fur. It felt soft as silk.

"I missed you. Would you come into the chalet?"

She nodded and got up. I liked seeing her in her wolf form. She mostly stays in her human form so seeing her like that was refreshing. I liked how she looked wild and strong. Yet, there was some sweetness in her eyes and in the way she cuddled with me. I could feel how she cared about me even in her wolf form.

I opened the door and Kate entered the chalet. I heard a noise as I closed the door and when I turned back, Kate was on the floor in her human form, naked.

"Oh my gosh you are magnificent!" I told her with a husky voice. She looked at me with lust in her eyes.

"I missed you so much!" she told me with a flirtatious voice.

A low purr escaped my chest as I watched her getting dressed. "It was better when you were naked, but you are still gorgeous."

Kate laughed at my praise as I hugged her lovingly. It felt so great to be able to appreciate the warmth of her body against mine. I missed her so much, I never wanted to let go of her.

"Finally, I get to have you in my arms," I whispered in her ear.

A soft purr resonated through her chest up into mine. She looked at me with a loving smile. "Finally, I have you all for myself," she told me voluptuously. We stayed like that for a moment, while I whispered sweet nothings into her ear and showered her with kisses.

I took her hand into mine. "Come," I told her as I walked her through each room, showing her our new home. For me, this was just a chalet, compared to the castle where I was used to live. But Kate looked like she was impressed, and I couldn't be happier. I wanted her to be happy here. I wanted her to like it so much she would like to stay forever.

All rooms were decorated with taste. It was comfortable and warm with a touch of luxurious but not too much.

I finished the tour with our bedroom. Kate noticed right away the dress that I had left on the bed for her.

"What's that?" she asked, curious.

"A gift for you. Tonight, we are celebrating *us*," I replied with a smirk on my face.

"Can I really wear a dress that pretty?"

Was she really asking this? I mean she was way prettier than that dress. I didn't really know how to make her see what I was seeing through my eyes when I looked at her.

"I tried to find a dress that matched your beauty, but I couldn't find anything that comes remotely close to you, so I hope you'll find it good enough to wear it."

Kate put a hand on her mouth as she gasped.

"Oh Damien! That's one of the most romantic things someone has ever told me."

I smiled, satisfied with the impact my words had on her. Nothing matched her beauty, I wanted her to see it. Maybe now she was closer to understanding how I felt about her.

"This dress is gorgeous! Of course, I'll wear it." She added with the biggest smile.

There was a small round table on the corner of the room. I had set up two wine glasses on it. A bottle of white sparkling wine was sitting in a bucket of ice, waiting for us.

Kate had a sparkle in her eyes as she spotted the drinks.

"Care to join me for a drink?"

She giggled a little. "Of, course!" she answered.

I poured the wine into the glasses, and we took a seat outside on the balcony, relaxing under the sun as the day passed by.

Kate looked at me, excited.

"I haven't told you yet! Guess what? The potion you gave me, it worked! My sister awoke!"

She had the biggest grin on her face. Anything that would make her happy would make me happy as well, if only to see her smile.

I winked at her. "What do you know? Guess that old sorcerer proved to be useful after all."

Kate laughed at my remark.

"How is she?"

"She's doing well. It turns out a demon was holding her prisoner with a curse. Eurynomos is his name, ever heard of it?"

I thought a little, back to my history classes. It's been a while, but I remembered this name.

"Yes, there's an old legend. They say the goddess Hecate is the goddess of vampires. She is the goddess of magic, witchcraft, ghosts and many more. She was the holder of keys, guardian of the gates of the underworld. She was capable of both good and evil. It is said that one day, she decided to let Eurynomos pass the gates from the underworld and let him enter our world."

Kate looked pensive.

"Huh, I guess that's when our legend comes in, then."

I looked at her with inquisitive eyes.

"It is said that Selene, the moon goddess, sealed Eurynomos in a sepulcher a very long time ago. But a few years ago, some werewolves freed him from the sepulcher. It was my mother and father who defeated him."

Huh, that's intriguing. I thought all those legends were only, well, legends. I never thought there could be some truth to all of this.

As I pondered to myself, Kate continued, "and you know what I learned? I thought my mother was only human. It turns out she was the moon goddess's daughter! But it seems that she's not anymore. The moon goddess's daughter is now my sister."

So many things to take in at the same time.

"Wait what? Your mother is the moon goddess's daughter? And so, is your sister?"

Kate laughed at all my questions.

"Yeah, it is quite a lot to take in, right? And none of this makes sense, but it's the best explanation we have so far."

She took a tone like she was explaining something to a kid and started from the beginning.

"It would seem that my mother was the moon goddess's daughter, but that she passed on those genes to my sister when she gave birth to her."

"Like, is this even possible?"

Kate shrugged her shoulders.

"I don't know, but it seemed that Eurynomos put a curse on the moon goddess's daughter years ago. Now that my sister has found her mate, the curse activated. Thus, the reason she was unconscious for a few days."

I was astounded by her story. As unlikely as it seemed, I must admit that what happened to her sister was strange. And since Elwin said that the magic that cursed her was stronger than the vampire lord's magic, I guess the fact that a demon was the source of the curse made sense. Still, it was quite a lot to take in.

By now, my drink was long empty, and I knew I needed another one to keep going through her story.

I asked Kate, "do you want me to get you another drink before we continue this story?"

Kate smiled at me and nodded. "That's a great idea!"

I brushed a soft kiss on her lips as I took her empty glass and went to fill our glasses.

As I made my way back to the balcony, I noticed the sun was already lower in the sky as it was already late afternoon.

I sat back in my chair and began to sip my drink.

"Okay, let's say that your mother was but is not anymore, the moon goddess's daughter. And let's say that your sister is now the moon goddess's daughter. How is it that she can talk to Eurynomos?"

Kate explained, "Bianca said that when she was asleep, her soul was taken prisoner by Eurynomos, in the realm where he is."

"I guess that would be the underworld."

She nodded. "But you see, all the while her soul was imprisoned, my sister was able to talk with Eurynomos. And what's more, she's not free yet. A part of her soul is still imprisoned. Until she is free, Eurynomos is able to see and hear everything my sister hears, and vice versa."

My heart sank at that last part. Her sister still isn't free from the demon. That can't be good. My little wolf will never be able to be completely happy if we can't manage to free her sister.

"What do we need to do to free her?"

Kate seemed to hesitate as she spoke.

"Well … it seems that vampires and werewolves need to associate themselves in order to free her."

Kate looked sad when talking about this. I wanted to cheer her up. I cupped her chin with my hand and raised her head so she would look into my eyes.

"Don't lose hope, my little wolf. We will stop this war, and we will get your sister free. You're talking to the heir of the throne, do not forget that! We'll make the impossible possible."

Kate's smile reappeared on her face. Her eyes sparkled with excitement once again as she spoke.

"Yes! You are right! And my brother said that he will accept you as my mate and that he wants to start over on the right foot with you."

I smiled at her words. That was good to hear, especially since I fought twice already with her brother.

She continued, "Everybody wants to help us stop the war! We're not alone in this."

"That is awesome! My brother will also help us. So, we're getting stronger, this is good."

Things were finally beginning to turn to our favor. At least it looked that way. I wanted to think it was, anyway. Now if only her uncle could find the book of vampires, we'd have a chance at stopping this war. Would stopping the war be enough to free Kate's sister? I certainly hoped so.

I looked up at my watch. It was time for supper already. I had planned a beautiful evening for Kate. I intended to make her feel like the princess she was meant to be. She was my partner, and as I was the heir to the throne, technically, she was a princess, although I have never officially proposed to her.

Kate looked at me as I stood up. Extending my arm to her, I asked, "would you care to join me for supper, my lady?"

Kate giggled at my question. "Of course, I will join you, my prince." She winked at me.

I led her to our bedroom and pointed to the dress on the bed.

"I will be waiting for you downstairs," I told her with a gentle tone. I left the room to let her change her clothes.

I was wondering how she would look in the dress I had chosen for her. It was a black lace, backless dress. I prepared our meal while I waited for her to come downstairs. I couldn't wait to see her. I hoped she would enjoy our evening.

This evening was meant only for her and me. Our first real evening as lovers. Thinking only of us and nothing more. The first time I could enjoy being with her, without fearing something would happen to her. The first night I'll be able to just taste her and appreciate her, savoring her for as long as I can before giving myself to the slumber of the night.

I stopped and turned as I heard some steps on the hardwood floors. She was even more stunning than I had imagined. I couldn't move as I was blown away by her beauty. I looked at her from head to toe.

"Wow," was all that I could get out, I was speechless.

I grabbed her hand and kissed it gently.

"You are stunning, my love," I whispered.

Kate blushed a little at my compliment. I walked her to the table and pulled the chair out for her. I held her waist gently as she sat down and pushed her chair to the table.

She was the most precious woman in the world.

I brought a fine bottle of red wine and poured a glass for her. Then I brought one of the finest bottles of blood wine and poured a glass for myself.

I raised my glass. "A drink to us. May our love stay strong and withstand the test of time."

Kate raised her glass, and we made a toast to our love.

I went to get our plates in the kitchen. Kate looked impressed as I had prepared delicious filet mignon platters. I chose only the finest ingredients to make her meal.

I grinned, happy to see Kate close her eyes and hum in delight as she ate the food. I wanted this meal to blow her away. Meals at the castle were always delicious. But preparing a meal for the one I love and seeing her enjoy it was way better.

We emptied our plates while talking and drinking our wine. We finished the meal with chocolate mousse. This supper was simply perfect.

We finished our glasses, and I could see the wine was having its effect on Kate as her cheeks were getting red and she had sultry eyes. I could say the wine influenced me too, as I could barely resist taking her now.

I took her hand and led her to the terrace outside where I had set up some soft lights and music. In her dress, she truly looked like a princess, and this was the perfect ballroom.

"May I have this dance?" I asked with a flirtatious smile.

Kate kissed me languidly and I noticed her body was even hotter than usual. I don't know if it was from that kiss of hers, the way she smelled or the way her breasts pressed against me as we kissed but I was getting rather aroused.

"I would love to."

That smirk of hers showed that she knew exactly what she was playing at and god I loved playing with her!

We danced to a few songs, the stars already lighting the skies, our bodies moving in sync. As the songs passed, Kate was getting naughtier and lustful. She would dance and make sure that her hips brush against my bulge every time I swirled her. She was toying with me and it felt so good. I could barely hold myself and I knew she wanted the same.

The songs succeeded themselves, but we barely listened to them. I kept following Kate's body as she moved. The moon was already high in the sky.

At one point, I couldn't take it anymore. I grabbed her hand and led her inside, to the bedroom, where she followed me willingly, with a seductive smile. I laid her carefully on the bed and started to slowly glide the straps of her dress down her shoulders, kissing her bare skin on my way. Kate moaned as I nibbled tenderly at her neck.

Kate started to run her fingers through my hair. I loved the way she tugged at it playfully. I let my hands roam freely on her body. I loved the way I made goosebumps appear on her skin to my heart's desire. Once in a while, when I brushed a sensitive spot, I would get rewarded with a moan from her that just made me desire her even more.

Kate started kissing my neck. I felt her warm breath on my skin and the tip of her fingernails graze at my neck, sending shivers down my spine. I could feel her heartbeat rising and her body's temperature increase as she was getting aroused. She started licking at my neck and I let out a groan as pleasure hit me when she licked the bite mark. It's as if my whole body was reacting at the mate mark she left me. As if my body just knew she was the one and was reacting to her touch.

I was overwhelmed with desire for her. Since she bit me the other day, I've been feeling this urge that was building inside. It was at its peak tonight, and I couldn't hold it in anymore. I undressed myself, finally getting myself free from those restrictive pants. Kate caressed my chest, I knew she liked my muscles, I could see it in her eyes every time she looked at me. I let her roam my body with her fingers as I removed the remainder of her clothes.

I kissed her passionately, our tongues dancing with each other. She was already wet with anticipation as I inserted a finger into her opening, making her gasp. She couldn't hold in her moans as I licked her clit. Her sweet moans made me want her even more, it sounded like a sweet paradise. She arched her back from pleasure as I ate her pussy. Her breaths were quickening as pleasure was building up.

I made my way back up, kissing her soft skin on my way. She grabbed my finger and started to lick it languidly. Every flick of her wicked tongue made me moan and ignited the fire within me even more.

She started to thrust her hips, letting me know she wanted more. I wanted her so bad, but I wanted to play with her more. So, I kept kissing every part of her soft skin, gliding my tongue across her skin.

"Oh, please Damien! Take me!" she asked me, pleading.

Her words aroused me even more.

"Hmmm, I like it when you beg me."

This could be a game I would play for a long time, I thought to myself.

By now I desired her so much. I lined myself with her. Kate groaned hard as I penetrated her while licking her nipples. She was so warm and slick for me, I moaned loudly. Thrusting softly and then hard, adjusting myself to her cries. She clawed at my back with her nails at the point where it stung a little.

As waves of pleasure hit us, my instincts were taking control of me, and I ended up brushing my teeth at her neck without even thinking about it. I hesitated, then backed from her neck. She grabbed my hair and pushed me back against her neck, begging me, "do it."

That was all the encouragement I needed. My body was calling me to take *all* of her. I sank my teeth into her neck, making her gasp from pleasure as I bit her. The feeling was just incredible. I felt like I was one with her, like I could feel her heartbeat inside of me. No words can properly explain this connection I was feeling right now. I drank her blood slowly, pacing myself. Her blood tasted like the sweetest nectar that ever existed, like it was made especially for me. I could never grow tired of her.

I didn't want to stop, but I didn't want to drink too much blood from her. I carefully removed my teeth from her neck, making the wound heal as I let my tongue linger where I had bitten. I thrust hard into her, making her scream my name. She was getting tighter and tighter. It was getting hard to resist but I didn't want it to end.

I felt her body tremble under me, her hands grasping my shoulders and her back arching against me as she screamed from pleasure. It was the perfect sight, and I loved the way she would tighten around me. I continued my endeavor, letting her come over and over again, watching her writhe and moan under me. Seeing her like that, I couldn't hold myself anymore as I let myself surrender to pleasure as I climaxed in my turn.

Finally, exhausted, we stayed together in each other's arms, basking in our love.

I've spent so many nights alone, thinking about her. But tonight, I was getting to keep her in my arms, finally.

As we laid in bed, I whispered to her, "I'm so madly in love with you, and yet, I know tomorrow I'll love you even more."

Kate smiled looking genuinely happy. "My life changed forever the day when you became a part of it. I couldn't be happier to have you as my mate. I love you so much Damien."

I hugged her tight in my arms enjoying her sweet scent. Her hair felt so soft. I felt a soft purr coming out of her chest, resonating within me, lulling me slowly. I kissed her tenderly. "Good night, my little wolf."

She whispered back, "good night, my love."

I felt her fall into a deep slumber as I caressed her back with my hand. This moment was my paradise. I didn't want to get to sleep, I wanted to enjoy this longer. In the end, I couldn't resist and fell asleep as well, holding the woman I loved in my arms.

Chapter 17 (Kate)

The journey to the valley

These past few days felt like a dream. Getting to spend my days with Damien, enjoying his company, seeing his personality. Finally, I was able to sleep in his arms. For a moment, I felt like all of my troubles went away. Nothing mattered anymore, not the war, not freeing my sister, the only thing that mattered was my mate.

In his arms, I felt safe and protected. His smile made my heart skip a beat and his kisses gave me butterflies.

I was enjoying myself, relaxing in Damien's arms, kissing his neck, and passing my fingers through his hair. Everything was just fine. Suddenly there was a knock on the door. I opened the door to see Will standing there. Behind him were Bianca and Steven.

"Hey Will, what brings you here?"

They entered the chalet, and I closed the door behind them. Damien stood up to meet them. Bianca's eyes widened. "Oh! I finally get to meet your mate!" she exclaimed herself.

I giggled at her comment as I went to Damien's side. He put his arm around my waist and kissed me on the cheek.

I made the official presentations. "Everyone, meet Damien, my mate."

Bianca jumped at Damien's neck and hugged him, taking him by surprise. I laughed a little, it was so her type to do that.

"Oh my gosh! I'm so happy to meet you!" she exclaimed as she took a step back.

"Damien, this is my sister Bianca, and her mate Steven."

Steven held out his hand to Damien.

"I heard you helped to break my mate's curse. I will forever be grateful to you!"

Damien smiled at him and grabbed Steven's hand, looking genuinely happy.

Will stayed behind, observing. He looked a little nervous, maybe from their previous encounters. I grabbed him gently by the arm and nodded.

"Damien, this is my brother, Will."

The two men looked at each other with respect. They seemed to understand each other through their gaze. Will took a step closer to Damien.

"It's nice to finally meet you properly," he said with a smile.

"Likewise," replied Damien, giving him a pat on the back.

It was really nice to see my brother and my mate finally getting along. I couldn't be happier. I looked at my brother.

I asked them, "what are you all doing here? Did you miss me?"

Will's face turned from happy to looking troubled. I had the feeling this was not good.

"I'm afraid that's not the reason we came here. Our lookouts have seen vampires marching towards the valley of Nysa. They say there is a lot of them. Mom and dad have set forth to meet them there, with all of the pack and our allies. The war is about to start."

I looked at my brother in shock, then at Damien. The valley of Nysa was the place where the war between vampires and werewolves occurred thousands of years ago. After the war, bodies were piled up everywhere in the valley. But since then, nature has taken over and the valley is now a luxurious plain of plants and grass. It is said that it is now the lands of wood nymphs.

"History is about to repeat itself... They're going to wage war at the same place it happened years ago," I said in dismay.

Will was about to say something but was interrupted by a knock at the door. I wondered who it could be, since Will, Bianca and Steven were already here.

I went to open the door, hoping it could be Zach, but I came face to face with Damien's brother.

"Oh, hi," I said, surprised.

After he saved my life, I knew that I could trust him. It's been a while since I saw him.

He looked surprised to see me answer the door, but he was smiling, running his hand through his hair.

He replied, "hey, glad to see you. I was expecting my brother to answer."

"So glad to see you!"

I gave him a hug. I guess I took him by surprise, but he hugged me back after a second or two.

Then he looked inside the chalet. "Looks like you are having a party but didn't invite me."

He smirked at his brother; Damien motioned for him to enter.

As Arius entered a silence fell upon the room, everyone stared at him.

"Everyone, meet my brother Arius," Damien said. "He is an ally."

Everybody relaxed after Damien said that last sentence.

Arius looked at his brother and made a remark, smiling. "Well, it seems that you make friends rather easily."

Damien laughed. "Well, it seems that having a werewolf as a mate comes with a lot of friends. Not that I'm complaining, I'm happy to have them as friends."

It filled my heart with joy to hear him say that.

Damien asked Will, "it seems we are missing one person; Zach is not here with you?"

My brother shook his head. "Nobody's seen him for the past few days. One morning he said something about a book and left. I have no idea where he is."

The book... So, it seemed that Zach was still searching for it. Maybe he remembered something. I hoped he would find it, and that it wouldn't be too late when he does.

"I guess we'll have to do without him, then," Damien replied.

Arius cut in the conversation. "I'm sorry to interrupt, but I am rather in a hurry. I came here because Father has summoned you, Damien. As heir prince, he wants you on the battlefield and was furious when he couldn't find you this morning."

A dead silence fell upon us. I looked to the floor, heartbroken at the thought of my mate being on the battlefield.

Damien's face hardened. "It seems we cannot avoid this war after all... I will go to the battlefield. I'm still hoping we can cut short the war and minimize casualties."

I grabbed Damien in my arms. "Please, don't go! I couldn't bear if something were to happen to you."

Damien hugged me tight. I hid my face in the crook of his neck, breathing his sweet scent. He backed me away just enough so I could look at him in the eyes. His gray eyes were full of love.

"I love you with all that I am, with all of my soul. If I don't go, my father will kill me. At least on the battlefield, I have a chance."

A few tears rolled on my cheeks, but Damien wiped them as they appeared.

"Then I will also go," I told him.

Damien shook his head. "Please, I don't want anything to happen to you."

My mind was set. If my mate were to be in this war, then I would be too. Whatever it would take, I would protect him. Surely, I would find a way to stop the war.

I replied, "if you are to be on the battlefield, then so will I."

Damien looked at me, he knew there was nothing he could do to make me change my mind.

Bianca added, "and so will we! There's no way we'll leave all the fun to you guys. We'll watch your backs."

I watched from afar. Darkness surrounded me. In the distance, I heard the rivers flowing and the lamenting of souls. This was my domain. I was the master here.

I looked at the soul fragment still imprisoned in the cage I set. I loathed her so much. There's no way I'll ever let her free. They can try to stop the war as much as they want. They are pathetic creatures. I can't wait to see their hope get crushed. They are fools to even think they can achieve peace.

I looked around the room. Everybody seemed to have their minds set on going to the war. My brother and Steven were amongst the best fighters of the pack. I hoped they would prevail. I was more worried about Bianca. She couldn't turn into a wolf... But it seemed she was the moon goddess's daughter. I didn't really understand exactly what this meant, but I hoped it came with some perks to help her during the war.

I looked at my sweet Damien, my love. I knew he could fight, and I knew vampires possessed many powers. I just hoped he would be strong enough not to get hurt. As I understood, the vampire Lord was the strongest of the vampires, then his wife. So, as the first prince, he was third in strength amongst the vampires. Surely, he would be able to fight, right?

Lastly, I watched Arius, I knew he was an ally. With him being second prince of the vampires, I hoped his strength would help us.

I hoped he could protect his brother. I cannot lie, my main concern was for Damien to make it unharmed in this war. If my mate were to die, I would be crushed forever.

My brother put his hand on Damien's shoulder. "I shall watch your back, but please, watch for my sister's safety."

Damien nodded. "Her safety is my main concern. I would give my life for her."

Will seemed happy with his answer.

"Stop it you two! Nobody's going to die today, okay?" I shouted at them, angry. "Stop talking like it's the last time we will see each other!"

Everybody laughed after what I said. At the same time, I think we all knew that nobody was safe during a war.

We all walked northeast, towards the valley of Nysa. Everyone seemed lost in their thoughts. We climbed on a small hill. Arrived at the top, we could see Nysa's valley in all its splendor.

The valley was topped with mountains on either side. From the tops of the mountains flowed rivers, which descended to the forests that lay at the base of the mountains. Finally, between the two mountains stood the large valley full of greenery.

On the left side of the valley stood the werewolves' army. Humans mixed with werewolves. Most of them were in their human form, but some of them were in their wolf's form. There were a few hundred of them. It looked like mom and dad rallied most of the packs in the area.

With them, it seems that the wood nymphs that reside in the valley decided to join the battle as well. I wondered why they would join the war as nymphs are usually passive creatures. Maybe to defend their homelands? I guess the war was invading their territory and it was a reason enough to fight for it.

The front line was composed of our Betas and our strongest fighters.

My parents stood in front of them all, representing the werewolves. They stood tall and strong facing the enemy's army.

On the right side stood the vampires' army. They seemed to match the werewolves' army in number. Within them were horned women, I guess they were succubi. I hated these deceitful creatures.

Looking at their front line, I recognized Lilith. She wore a large armor and wielded a long sword. She stood tall and strong. Her eyes were full of hate for her enemies. Other vampires were with her on the front line. It looks like all the strongest of the fighters were there. I recognized the assassins that attacked me the other day as well.

At the front of them stood a man and a woman. I guess it was the vampire lord and the vampire queen. Damien's parents. I've never met them, but they looked strong. The man had long white hair and looked to be very powerful; it looked like an aura of magic emanated from him. No wonder everyone feared him … including his own sons.

The woman had very long brown hair and looked graceful. She had the same gray eyes as Damien. She seemed to be powerful too. It looked like she had more control over her powers as she seemed better at containing them than her husband. Damien looked a lot like his mother.

Overall, the two armies looked to be equally strong, and the battle would be a test of strengths for sure. That scared me a lot, because it also meant that there would be casualties on both sides, and I didn't want anything to happen to Damien or to anyone I loved.

I turned to Damien; I was getting rather worried about the events to come. Doubts started to fill my mind. What if we couldn't stop them? What if we were to get hurt? Could I protect my mate? Could I protect my brother and sister? All of a sudden, everything just became so much more real...

I felt the heat rise on my cheeks; a lump formed in my throat as I suppressed a few sobs.

Damien turned to me. "Are you alright, my little wolf?" he asked, his voice full of concern.

"I'm scared," I told him, which was true.

He hugged me tenderly. "I know it's okay my love. We'll get through this."

In his arms I felt a little better. I wanted this moment to last, I didn't want to get to the war.

Couldn't we just let them fight each other and stay out of it?

My conscience would not let me do that. I loved all my family. I had to try to stop the war, even though we risked our lives.

I turned to everyone. "They haven't started fighting yet. Maybe there's still a way to stop them."

Will answered, "yes, but Zach is still not here with the book. I don't know how we'll stop it."

We all looked at each other. I think nobody really knew how we could stop the war.

"It doesn't matter!" said Damien with determination. "We'll find a way. Together we can do this."

He sounded so confident. I think he gave us hope.

"Is everybody ready?" I asked.

They all nodded.

We did a group hug and started to get down the hill to go join the armies. We were still far and neither army saw us yet. I wondered what they would think if they noticed us. A group of werewolves and vampires together.

As we got down the hill, my parents started to walk towards the vampires. The vampire lord and queen did the same. A silence fell in the valley as leaders of both armies prepared to talk together. They were still a few yards one from another, so they had to speak loudly enough for each other to understand.

Although we were still far, we could still hear them, as the sound of their voice was resonating on the rock walls up to us.

"We stand here today because you have broken the peace treaty!" my father said.

"Nonsense!" replied the vampire Lord. "You broke the peace treaty first."

Even from afar the tension was palpable between them.

My father retorted, "you entered our territory, attacked us and kidnapped my daughter! How dare you accuse us of breaking the peace treaty?"

The vampire lord grinned. "The treaty has been broken from a far longer time than this and you know it! Stop playing innocent!"

It was frustrating to see them argue about this. My father had no idea about the book so, of

386

course, he couldn't know what the vampire lord meant. And the vampire lord was sure that werewolves stole it. They were both right from their point of view. Yet in truth, they were both wrong. If only I could show them the truth.

Each leader was waiting for the other one to admit their fault, waiting for the other to show weakness.

We were running as fast as we could down the hill. As we reached a distance where maybe we would have a chance of them hearing us, the vampire lord stated, "so be it."

Both my parents and Damien's parents bowed slightly as they backed up to their original positions.

We tried to get their attention, to scream at them, but the war drums had started to sound on both sides of the armies, making any attempts to talk to them futile. Warriors were getting ready on both sides. Succubi were deploying their wings, preparing to take flight, to attack from the skies. Wood nymphs were warming up their magics, spawning magic balls, sprouting roots at strategic places, ready to grab the ankles of enemies passing by. Some of the werewolves were turning to their wolf forms. Vampires were growing out their fangs and sharpening their nails. Some of them taking flight, others staying on foot.

You could feel the adrenaline rushing to the beat of the drums. Everyone on their toes, just waiting for the final signal to be given. Finally, with the leaders back at their leading spots, the war horns were blown on each side and the two armies started charging towards each other.

I fell to my knees as I watched in disarray my family fight against Damien's family. I felt despair take hold of my heart, as I knew people I loved risked being torn apart by a useless war. I felt so helpless. Tears ran down my cheeks to the ground.

Two strong arms rested on my shoulders. I looked up to see Damien's gray eyes gazing at me. He offered me his hand. I grabbed it and he raised me in his arms.

"Come, my little wolf. Let me see that fire in you that I love so much. I know it's in there somewhere."

This was so much to take in, I didn't know if I had what it took to deal with it. Although, I knew deep down he was right. I looked into his eyes, looking at my reflection, searching for an answer.

In his eyes, I saw fear, but I also saw love, hope, and … our future together. This was it. It was the time to get our future. This was our chance at being mates. It was a chance to grasp, even though it came with risks. We had to get out there, and stop this war, whatever the consequences.

As I looked at him, he started to smile.

"That's more like it." He grinned.

"Thank you for reminding me of who I am. I'm a fighter. We'll get through this, we'll stop this war. After that, we'll get to live together."

I hugged him into my arms, savoring his love and scent. It was like taking a breath of air before dipping into the darkness of the waters without knowing if you'll have the opportunity to take another one.

I reached for his mouth, kissing him passionately, our tongues dancing together as he caressed my back. As we parted, he told me, "now and forever, I'll always love you."

My heart fluttered at his words as I answered, "No matter what happens, my heart will always be yours."

Now sure more than ever of what must be done, we finished our descent to join the armies. We mustn't give up.

Chapter 18 (Kate)

The war

By the time we arrived at the battle; everyone was in a big melee, fighting. Succubi were attacking from the sky, trying to grab wood nymphs or smaller wolves in their talons. Wood nymphs sent magic balls at vampires and grew roots to hold still their enemies in place, working in teams to defeat them.

Vampires were attacking the werewolves at godlike speed. Their magic was more powerful than most of the werewolves' magic. Humans from our packs had put on armors and wielded silver swords against vampires. They were the more at risk in this war, as they had no particular powers compared to all the other races. But humans made up in ingenuity what they lacked in strength.

Werewolves attacked in groups, biting the flesh of their enemies or tearing their skin with their sharp claws. Some of them in their human form testing their strength with bare arms against vampires.

One had to be careful as bites came from succubi, vampires and werewolves at the same time. In the heat of the battle, one could not be completely sure the bite would hit a friend or a foe. Blood was already spilling on the grass of the valley, tainting flowers, and forming small puddles in some areas.

Together, we decided to try to get to the lord and queen who were fighting with my parents. Steven and Bianca were already further ahead.

I was trying to catch up to them when suddenly a sharp pain hit me. I felt sharp nails in my back and teeth sink into my shoulders. I tried to look back to see my attacker and caught a glimpse of red hair. I didn't really have to look, as I could recognize her cheap perfume smell anywhere. That bitch was taking her revenge.

I tried to shake her free, but she was out of reach on my back, and I was having difficulty.

I heard a powerful shout, "Ellie, let go of her! Now!"

The vampire on my back hissed at Damien. There was no way she was releasing me. I could feel it through the force she was applying. Her nails were digging deeper in my skin, blood dripping from the wounds. She wanted me dead. Maybe she thought she could have her boyfriend back if she killed me?

I was getting dizzy from the pain. I called to my mate in my mind, "Damien, please."

I didn't have to ask another time as Damien jumped on Ellie. She screamed in surprise, as she released her hold on me. I stumbled to my feet and watched them fight.

"You would fight your own kind?" Ellie hissed in disbelief.

"I will fight whoever threatens my mate." Damien snarled at her, before lunging an attack, sending her on the ground a few feet away.

"You should know better than to fight a prince, if you know what's good for you."

He warned her as she lay on the ground. He slowly walked towards her, looking menacingly at her.

Ellie got back up, hissed at him. She looked like she was weighing her options. Finally, she decided to run away, disappearing in seconds at the far end of the battle.

"Thanks," I told him.

He nodded at me. My back was hurting as well as my neck. The wound didn't seem too serious. It would surely heal soon. There was no time. I turned back to make my way in the direction of the leader's fight. This was our only chance to stop this war.

*********** Damien's POV ***********

At least she was safe. I never thought Ellie would do something as bold as to try to kill my mate. I should've given her a bigger punishment than that. I would have if we weren't in the middle of a war. I'll take a mental note to get back to her after all of that is finished. No one threatens the woman I love and gets away with it.

395

I didn't even have the time to follow Kate to get to my parents that I got attacked by three werewolves at the same time. One biting my arm, another at my leg and the other one trying to get at my neck. All of them were trying to get me to trip down so they could get on top of me on the floor.

I was strong and although I didn't really want to hurt them, I couldn't let myself get hurt. I fought back one of the wolves, throwing him on the ground. But it seemed that every time I got one off of me, another one jumped on me. I guess teamwork really does payoff.

I sent a wave of my power all around me, sending them all at once to the ground. They circled me, growling. There was now six of them, just waiting for an opportunity to take me down.

"Don't you attack," a stern voice said. Will arrived with perfect timing. He made his way through the wolves and came to my side.

"He might not be a wolf, but he is an ally. That vampire you see right now just saved your future Alpha, my sister."

The wolves stopped, they watched me intensively. Then, as if they had made up their minds, they nodded their heads in our direction and went away.

I turned to Will. "Thanks! You really saved me."

He grinned. "Thanks for saving my sister." He patted me on the back.

Arius arrived, out of breath. "Are you guys, okay?"

Will and I nodded to him.

We turned our heads to hear a familiar voice. Steven and Bianca were a little further, overrun by vampires. Steven tried to protect Bianca to his best and Bianca did her best to fight them off, but there were too many of them.

Arius and I nodded at each other and jumped into the melee, to protect them. Together, we were two of the most powerful vampires; surely, we would have no problem handling them.

************ Kate's POV ************

I was near my parents. I could feel an overwhelming power coming from their battle with the vampire lord and queen. I turned around to check if the others were following me, but to my surprise, they weren't there.

I screamed, "Mom! Dad! You have to stop!"

Neither of them heard me, or if they did, they ignored me.

I tried to get to them, but Lilith appeared in front of me, stopping me.

"It seems we meet again," she spoke in a calm voice.

"Please… I know you are not like that. I remember your smile. I remember how you were. You loved him and he loved you. Please don't do this."

"That person is long dead."

She replied, her eyes full of hate and sadness.

Slowly, she began to close the distance between us. She had a menacing look, and I was getting scared. I hoped I wouldn't have to fight her.

"You will pay the price of your treachery," she told me with an icy stare.

"I didn't even do anything!" I pleaded.

But she would not stop, coming slowly but surely to me, with murderous eyes. I knew she was Zach's mate, but at the same time, I wouldn't let myself be killed.

"Lilith, stop!" a voice yelled from behind me.

That voice, I could recognize it anywhere. It seems Lilith recognized him as well.

Zach ran to my side, out of breath. "I came as fast as I could."

In his hands, he held a deerskin satchel covered with dirt.

Lilith shouted at him, "You betrayed me!"

"No … no please my love, listen to me," Zach tried to explain.

"Don't you dare call me like that! You left me alone all those years! You tricked me! You have no right to call me your love anymore."

Through her eyes, I could see the hurt she had inside, boiling and eating her from inside. All that pain was resurfacing with the arrival of Zach. She was right, he had no right to call her love after all those years left alone. Even if he didn't hurt her intentionally. Those things need time to heal.

I felt like I didn't belong in this conversation. Yet, there was no way for me to get away from it. I wanted to get to the lord and queen and stop the war, but Lilith was blocking my path.

Zach wasn't speaking, I think he had trouble finding the words, so I spoke first.

"He … couldn't come back to you," I told Lilith.

She looked at me without saying anything.

"When I tried to open the book, the curse activated. Because I'm not a vampire," Zach explained.

"What the heck are you talking about? What curse?" Lilith asked in disbelief.

"Have you ever heard of it? Damien told me a curse protects the book. A curse to preserve the secrets of the vampires. To make sure it never falls in the hands of someone who is not a vampire."

Zach continued, "the curse made me forget everything! I even forgot my heart's desires… It pains me so much… I am so sorry Lilith."

"Why would I believe you? You abandoned me! You tricked me to get our book and left me!"

Zach looked hurt.

"Please, Lilith. Please believe me. It wasn't like that at all."

"Have you no idea how much I've been hurt?"

Zach took a step towards her.

"I can't even imagine how much you must have hurt... But please, give me a chance to redeem myself. My love for you is unchanged. Please let me show you it was because of the curse."

Zach really looked sincere. Lilith's face softened, anger seemingly making place to astonishment and sadness as she comprehended what had happened. Of course, it would take some time for things to get back to the way it was between them, but at least the first step had been taken.

Zach looked hurt by everything that was happening, but he looked determined to carry on and fix things. He slowly opened the satchel he was holding, revealing a big book. The cover looked like it was made from different pieces of hide sewed together.

The book emitted a wave of magic as Zach got it out of the satchel, sending everybody that was close, including fighters, to the ground.

There was now an area of a few feet wide of calmness with no fight. Everybody on the ground, looking around them in astonishment.

Further on, everybody was still fighting. Fury raged all around us. It was as if we were in the calm of the eye of the hurricane.

My parent's and the vampire lord and queen's eyes turned on us. The vampire lord exclaimed, "here is the thief, at last!" pointing to Zach.

He looked angry, on the verge of assaulting Zach.

Lilith spoke, "he... He didn't steal it... I did."

The vampire lord asked, "what is the meaning of this?"

Zach walked to Lilith and took her gently in his arms. She accepted his hug, squeezed his arm in response and placed a kiss on his cheek. She then released herself from his embrace and took a step towards the vampire lord.

"He is my mate. I brought him the book years ago, in search of a way to expand his lifespan, in order to live with him for all of my life. But when he opened the book, the curse activated, and he forgot everything."

Zach added, holding out the book at the end of his arms. "I came to return it."

Lilith's voice was shaking as she spoke to the vampire lord. He had a stern look on his face.

"I'm sorry for taking the book without asking," she added, pleading the lord with her eyes.

The vampire lord looked furious.

He raised his hand and sent a bolt of energy in Lilith's way, but Zach pushed her out of the way and took the hit in her place.

Zach was sent flying to the floor a few feet away from the impact. The book of the vampire's secrets fell to the floor a few feet further.

"Zach," Lilith screamed, throwing herself to the floor at his side.

Lilith anxiously checked Zach's vital signs. She shielded his body with hers, crying.

I ran by her side. "Is he dead?"

She shook her head. "No, but he's barely alive. I wished for him to come back for so many years. And now that I get him back..." her voice broke as she couldn't finish her sentence.

I turned back to watch the vampire lord and queen.

Damien's mom looked furious.

"Orpheus! How could you? You would have killed my sister?"

She looked pissed. The vampire lord seemed to regret having angered his wife.

He didn't have time to reply anything. The group of succubi started to hover over the vampire lord. The lord's eyes shifted to the sky. All of a sudden, they all made to the ground at the same time, sending a wave of energy to the ground. The energy wave was strong enough to send Damien's mom and me, to the ground further.

The vampire lord was still standing, as he had an incredible force. "Oraya, how dare you attack me? I was the one who hired your group."

Oraya had a wicked smile. "My dear Orpheus, I just grew tired of this war, that's all. I figured I would have much more fun if I were to dispose of you," she said in a playful tone while licking her sharp teeth.

The vampire lord watched them thoughtfully. He was strong, but the succubi were strong demons too. There were five of them, and he was alone.

The succubi were circling Orpheus, waiting for him to make a move, studying him.

When finally, he decided to try to get at Oraya, the other succubi attacked him from behind and from the sides. He wouldn't have the upper hand in this battle, I could feel it.

I stood up, slightly dizzy but not hurt. Damien's mom did the same. I knew I was not as strong as they were, but I couldn't stay here and just watch. Against demons and succubi, my holy fire spear would surely prove useful. These were powerful opponents; it was worth using my inner power.

I concentrated as Ayanna told me, and soon enough, the flaming spear appeared in my hand. One of the succubi hissed as she looked at the weapon I wielded.

Damien's mom looked at me, surprised, but stood by my side and helped me fight against them.

Seeing their daughter fight, my parents decided to join, and started to attack another succubus.

We were fighting as much as we could, but Oraya, the leader of the group, succeeded in killing the vampire lord, ripping his flesh apart and drinking his blood. When they were done feasting on the lord's body, the other succubi turned their attention to us.

Luckily for us, Will, Arius, Steven and Bianca joined us in the fight. We were now eight against five. I swung my spear at them, it seemed pretty effective. In one big swing, I managed to behead the closest succubus. Together, we succeeded in killing another one rather quickly and scared the others enough that they decided to flee. I was happy they did, as I knew my weapon would soon disappear.

I didn't have time to say anything before my parents embraced me. They must have been scared of losing one of their daughters. I was happy to have them safe too, their embrace felt warm.

"I'm so proud of you, my daughter."

My father told me.

"Your inner power is impressive!"

I watched as I noticed his thickened skin.

"So is yours."

The vampire queen ordered the battle horn to be blown. Everyone stopped fighting. The war was over.

I looked around; bodies were lying around everywhere. Pools of blood formed in crevices in the ground. But at last, it was over.

I looked at Lilith, who was mumbling something to herself. I watched as she cut open her wrist with her nail, letting her blood drip inside Zach's mouth before healing her wound.

I went by her side and asked, "what are you doing?"

She looked at me. "Zach is gravely wounded. He will not survive. But I gave him my blood. Thanks to that, he will turn into a vampire. I am not losing him a second time."

She looked at him, her eyes full of love. Then she added with a smile.

"The best part is that he will now be a werewolf vampire, so he'll get to live for as long as I do."

She picked him up in her arms gently.

"I will bring him to my room and look after him. The transformation should take only a few days. We'll have all the time we need to work things out between us."

I nodded to her as I watched her walk away with my uncle in her arms. She looked happy and peaceful at last. I guess the mate bond is *that* strong. Even after all these years, she didn't give up on him. And now, they'll be able to fix what was broken and start anew.

I then turned to see if everyone else was okay.

Will was fine, he was with Bianca and Steven.

"I'm so happy that you're unharmed," Bianca told Steven.

Steven grinned at her and got the luck charm she gave him out of his pocket.

"Looks like the luck charm you made me kept me safe."

They all laughed, looking happy and relieved.

The vampire queen was mourning the loss of her husband. Arius was by her side, consoling her.

A knot formed in my stomach. I realized I hadn't seen Damien for quite some time now.

I asked Arius, "Have you seen Damien?"

He and the queen raised their eyes in my direction. Arius shook his head.

I looked up to Will, Bianca and Steven and asked them.

"Have any of you guys seen Damien?"

They all shook their heads.

"Who is Damien?" my mother asked.

I answered, "he is my mate."

Damien's mom put a hand on her mouth as I spoke those words.

I was beginning to panic, my heartbeat increasing. I tried not to think of everything that could have happened. I didn't want to jump to conclusions.

I tried to talk to Damien through our mate bond, but I couldn't communicate with him. What the hell was going on? Where was he? He was the heir to the throne, for god's sake! He was supposed to be strong.

Everyone started looking for Damien with me. I tried to concentrate on his scent, but there was too many bodies and blood everywhere. There was no way I could find his scent amongst all these smells.

After a few minutes, I finally spotted Damien, lying on the ground, inert.

"Damien!" I screamed as I ran to his body.

He was not moving. He can't be! I touched his body, but it was cold. Colder than his usual cool body temperature. His eyes were not opening and sure enough, he wasn't breathing.

Tears began to flow on my cheeks. How could this be? It can't be! I didn't even have time to really be with him yet!

My mother tried to get me away from him and take me into her arms, but I didn't let her. I didn't want to be away from my mate.

"No!" I screamed. It was a deep scream, mixed with a howl coming from my wolf.

I knew my family was there, watching me. Bianca in Steven's arms, crying. Will, watching me, helpless, with no way of consoling his sister. The vampire queen, now mourning both her husband and son, and Arius, trying to console her as best as he could.

All those times I needed him; he was there for me. He nursed me back to health. He saved my life. He was so kind to me, took good care of me, like a mate should. But I wasn't there to save him. What good is an inner power if in the end, you can't save the one you love?

I begged the moon goddess.

"Please, Selene, my goddess, please give me back my mate. We've worked so hard for us to be able to live together! The war is finally over. Please will you help me?"

Nothing could console me. I was hurting. My heart was broken. My wolf was hurting from the loss of her mate. It will take several days for her to fully recover from the loss of her mate. Even more so since the mating process was complete.

To think I could never hear his voice again. How I missed his delicious scent. I missed everything about him already.

I collapsed on Damien's body, sobbing. Grief fell upon me like an earthquake. It hit me, and my world fell apart. I know very well that even if I put my world back together, aftershocks are going to hit again, never really letting me get back to how I was before. The future that I've built in my head. My hopes, my dreams … all crushed.

I felt a warmth behind me. I turned around to see Bianca glowing white. A woman's voice came out of everywhere around us.

"You both helped my daughter quite a lot. Thanks to you and him, my daughter has awoken from the curse." The voice started, "I have pity on you, as you see, I am a goddess of kindness. And so, I shall grant you back your mate."

Was it really who I thought it was? Could this be really possible? I didn't dare to believe what I was hearing. I was afraid I was hallucinating or something. I looked around and sure enough, the others seemed to be hearing this too.

I watched in awe, as Bianca stopped glowing, returning to her normal self.

She looked like she was having a conversation with someone only she could hear.

Bianca took a few steps and kneeled at Damien's body. She hovered her hands on top of Damien and concentrated. A wind of energy started to flow from her hands. It was blowing around us, lifting Bianca's hair in the air. This lasted for a few seconds, before Bianca removed her hands and the wind died.

I was watching Damien, waiting, when I noticed his chest rising and lowering itself again. He was breathing!

*********** Damien's POV ***********

I opened my eyes slowly. I tried to think back to what had happened, but I couldn't; my mind was fuzzy. All of a sudden, I felt a warm embrace over me. It was her sweet scent; it was my love. I squeezed her tight, enjoying her warmth.

What had happened? Was the war over? I didn't understand. I looked at Kate, her eyes were red from crying. A little further, my mother was there, watching us, crying but smiling at the same time. Arius was there too, as well as Will, Bianca and Steven. At their side was a man and a woman, which I guessed where Kate's parents as they looked a lot like Kate and Will.

I had absolutely no idea what was going on. The only thing I knew is that I loved Kate with all of my heart. I cupped her face with my hand and kissed her. It felt so good, it felt like it's been ages since I've kissed her.

I sat up. "What happened? Why is everybody here? Is the war over?"

Kate didn't leave my side; she held my hand. I didn't know what had happened, but she needed to be with me right now.

My mother came and hugged me. "Oh my gosh, Damien, you were gone … you were dead."

Then she also hugged Kate.

I was dead? I couldn't believe this. It could certainly explain why Kate had cried. I looked at my brother, he nodded.

Bianca spoke. "The moon goddess gave you back your life, so you can live with your mate. It's her way to thank you for helping me, her daughter."

Was she serious? The moon goddess gave me back my life?

I looked at them, but they all nodded.

Then Bianca stepped forward towards us. "The moon goddess also said that I could grant you guys something else that you wished dearly."

I was wondering what she meant by that.

Then she looked at her sister.

"If you want to, I can expand your lifespan, so that you can live as long as your mate. Would you like that?"

That was too good to be true. It was all that I could have wished for.

Kate was crying from happiness as she nodded to her sister and hugged her.

Bianca wiped her tears and smiled. Then, she closed her eyes and placed her hands upon Kate. A white wind circled the two girls, as they began glowing bright for a few seconds, before dying down.

Bianca stated, "it is done."

Kate's parents came to hug us. "My daughter, I'm so happy that you've found your mate. What a lovely young man too."

Kate's mom said as she came to hug me.

Kate giggled, "mom, dad, meet Damien, my mate."

Then she looked at me, "Damien, meet my mom Sarah, and my dad Sam."

I looked at her parents. "It's an honor to meet you both."

I looked at Kate. She looked overwhelmed by everything that was happening.

If it's true that I was indeed dead as they say, then she had to feel the pain of losing me. I know I never wanted to live without her. I wanted to make sure we would stay together forever.

I took Kate's hand in mine, kneeling one knee on the ground.

"Kate, it seems that you had to go through the pain of losing me once already. I never want you to have to go through that pain again. Will you make me the luckiest man in the world, will you become my princess, and soon my queen? Will you marry me?"

Kate put her hands over her mouth as she nodded. "Yes! Oh my god Damien yes I will!"

She jumped into my arms and kissed me. I couldn't be happier.

My mother stood in front of the vampires, as she spoke with a strong voice.

"The lord died in the war. There will be a coronation in the next few weeks so that my son, Prince Damien, takes his rightful place as the new vampire lord, along with his queen, Kate."

So many things were happening at the same time. My father was dead?

I guess I would need to marry her soon then, to ascend to the throne with her. All the vampires around us cheered.

************ Kate's POV ************

I couldn't believe all that had just happened. It was just too much to take in at the same time and

I'm not really sure I realized the extent of everything yet. I knew that this was certainly both the worst and the happiest day of my life. Well, it was the worst day of my life when Damien died, but now, it was the happiest day of my life.

My wolf was happy knowing that not only my mate was alive, but also that I would get to live as long as him. I couldn't believe he proposed to me. This was just perfect.

And then, to think I would become the next vampire queen soon. This was all so much!

A question suddenly popped in my mind. I turned to my sister and asked her, "now that the war is over, are you finally free from Eurynomos?"

My sister shook her head. "It seems that it was not enough to free my soul completely from the demon."

That was disappointing, but only a setback. I wouldn't give up on her. Especially after she gave life back to my mate and extended my own lifespan.

"We'll find what it takes to free you, and do it," I told her with determination. I looked at Damien and he nodded.

Mom, dad, Will, Bianca and Steven returned to my parents' house. The werewolves' army returned to their pack's houses.

The wood nymphs got their territories back, although it's been partly destroyed but everyone agreed, both werewolves and vampires, they would come and help them rebuild and cleanup in the next few days.

The vampires also returned to their territory. As for me, it was decided that I should live with Damien, in the castle, to learn my future duties as queen. His mother had taken me under her wing and will show me all that I need to learn. This also meant that I would get to stay by Damien's side all the time, which was great. My wolf was still feeling uneasy at the idea of being apart from him.

Damien squeezed my hand, getting me out of my thoughts.

"Is something troubling you?"

Sincerely, I've never felt happier in my life. I smiled at him.

"No, everything is perfect, let's go home."

I rested my head on his shoulder as he embraced me tight. Before long, we were flying high in the sky to get back home to the castle.

Epilogue

Happy ever after ... or almost

************ Damien's POV ************

A lot of things had happened in the last few days. Being able to spend all my days with Kate seems like a dream come true. She has a lot of things to learn from my mother in a short amount of time, so I can't spend all the time that I want with her. And now that my dad is not here anymore, I have a lot of things to prepare also, in succeeding him. But still, I get to eat my meals in her company and get to hold her in my arms every night. *That* by itself is a blessing.

The book of vampires' secrets was now back into our sacred vault, where it's supposed to be. With the book returned, our armies cheered and accepted peace. Everyone accepted Kate as my fiancée easily even though she's not a vampire. I couldn't be happier, even more so that I knew now that her lifespan had been extended and that she would live with me for all of my life.

One of the first things we decided to do after we got back from the war, was to declare that vampires were free to visit werewolves and step in their territories, if they respected each other, and vice versa. It was allowed for our two kinds to be friends and we encouraged everyone to try to learn from one another. Kate and I had lots of plans to get an everlasting peace between werewolves and vampires. We hoped our people would understand each other better and learn one from another.

I was lost in my thoughts while I was getting prepared.

"You're not getting cold feet, are you?" a voice teased behind me.

It was Zach. Lilith had turned him to a vampire to save him from death. His transformation was now complete, but he was still learning to fully use his vampire's powers. He kept his wolf-shifting abilities, becoming the first vampire werewolf (to my knowledge). He looked more than happy to have been reunited with his mate.

I liked having him around. He instantly became my favorite uncle without even trying, as if he'd been part of my life since the beginning. And I was happy that Kate had her uncle living with us at the castle, as the rest of her family was living in the werewolves' territory.

I smiled at him as I adjusted my bow in the mirror. "Of course not!"

He wore a tuxedo, as did I. I asked him to be one of my best men. The other one being my brother.

"I'm not getting cold feet, but I have to admit I'm getting a little nervous."

Zach smiled at my answer. "It's going to be fine."

I knew he was right. He patted me on the back as my brother entered the room.

Together, we made our way to the ceremony.

Everybody was already there. We had invited a lot of werewolves on Kate's side. Sarah and Sam were there, as well as Will, Bianca and Steven. We also invited some of her best friends that I had never met before, some aunts and uncles.

All of my family was there on my side. My mother was looking fondly at me, already tearing up from the emotion. The back rows were filled with noble vampires and their family.

I looked strong and tall on the outside, smiling, but I was getting nervous.

I waited anxiously for Kate to arrive. I wondered how she would look. I'm sure she will be magnificent.

We didn't have a lot of time to prepare for the wedding but luckily, being a prince meant that I had a lot of people at my disposal to give tasks. Thanks to that, it looked like everything was prepared a long time ago. Bouquets of flowers everywhere letting their scent fill the room. White lace streamers were hanging from the ceiling, decorated with crystal.

My gaze fell on the carpet covered with rose petals where Kate will soon walk. I couldn't wait for her to come out. And I didn't have to wait long, as soon enough, the music started playing and Kate appeared under the arch, accompanied by her father.

She wore a white long, elegant dress that hugged her curves. The top of the dress was laced and strapless, letting the beautiful skin of her shoulders be seen. White flowers decorated her braided hair. And since she was now a princess, a small tiara completed the look.

She was even more stunning than I had imagined. I was in awe as I watched her walk the aisle with her father. He had a proud look on his face when he put his daughter's hand into mine.

*********** Kate's POV ***********

My heart was beating so fast. We turned to the priest and said, "I do." Although I already marked Damien as my mate, the wedding made it more official to everyone else, especially to vampires.

Damien cupped my face gently. I brought my lips to his. I had butterflies in my stomach. A spark ignited inside of me from Damien's touch as we kissed. Our tongues were dancing together as I couldn't have enough of him. We finally broke the kiss.

The priest spoke solemnly, "I present to you Prince Damien, our future lord, and Princess Kate, our future queen."

Everybody cheered and applauded. I blushed as I realized, I was now officially a princess. This all seemed unreal. I knew that in two weeks only I would need to take the role and responsibilities of a queen. But for now, I just wanted to enjoy this moment.

We made our way to the reception room. Moonbeams were entering through the large windows. The windowed doors of the room were open, and people could go out to the terrace to enjoy the night. Outside, lights were hanging from the pergola of the terrace.

Inside, at the center of the room was a big dance floor. Some people were still sitting at tables on the side of the room, others were standing, talking and watching us.

I danced a waltz with Damien in front of everyone. His eyes sparkled like the stars outside. Through our bond, I could feel completeness. I felt safe, loved and knew that I would never be alone again. Everyone soon joined us on the dance floor. The cook had baked us an outrageous cake. The food was excellent and so was the wine.

Damien and I were sitting at a table with my parents, his parents, my brother, sister and her mate. Everybody was having a good time. It seemed I would finally be able to relax a little with my mate and look forward to our future together. Maybe even think about having some pups together, who knows? I smiled at myself at that thought. I now had a few hundred of years ahead of me to enjoy my life with Damien.

Damned those wretched creatures! How could they stop the war? Rage flowed through my veins. This is meaningless! I still have the fragment of her soul. She's not free yet. Now's not the time to be fooling around. I can hear my army getting restless. I will strike before they can free her.

I took a look at my army. Centaurs, chimera and harpies by hundreds. Near the gate, orcs are forging weapons and getting prepared to break through. Soon... Very soon. We'll break through.

If that wretched goddess thinks she can keep me imprisoned here, she's mistaken.

Suddenly, Bianca rose, looking anxious. We all looked at her.

I asked her, "What is it?"

She answered, "there's an old gate, a gate to the underworld. The gate is rumored to be found at the bottom of a cave. Eurynomos is trying to open that gate to enter our world."

I gasped in surprise at her words and looked at Damien. He nodded at me.

I looked at everyone at the table. Zach and Lilith were just beside us, they also heard everything. Everyone had a serious look on their faces. We knew what needed to be done.

I guess my happily ever after will have to wait a little.

A word from the author

Hey!

I hope you enjoyed my book. I'm always happy to hear what you have to say about it, so don't forget to leave a review.

Check out my website and subscribe to my mailing list at daniellephauthor.com

The sequel, A Beloved Sin, is already available. Another steamy romance fantasy. This book will break you…

Discover what happens when love and death entangle themselves in a dangerous dance.

Get it today on Amazon.

Please leave a review on amazon and goodreads!

Thanks for your support

Danielle

Made in the USA
Las Vegas, NV
16 January 2023